AMONG TREACHEROUS STARS

THE TRAVELS OF SCOUT SHANNON

KATE MACLEOD

1

SCOUT SHANNON HAD NEVER BEEN off the surface of her home world before. She had never even been to the spaceport by the capital city, although she had been near enough to see the starry brightness of the rockets charging up into the sky. Once there had been many—or so she had been told—but since the war that had broken out before she was born, very few ships were launched up into orbit anymore, the domain of the Planet Dwellers' enemies, the Space Farers.

On the infrequent times when she had heard the low rumble of rocket engines, she'd always stopped wherever she was—usually on her bike making a delivery or carrying a message—and turned to watch the shimmering pinpoint of light rising up from the prairie. She remembered the rumble being so low it almost couldn't be heard, but she could feel it vibrating in her chest. Even kilometers away, she had felt the awesome power of a human-made machine battling gravity.

But until a few days ago, she'd never seriously thought about leaving her home world. Few Space Farers lived on the surface, and even fewer Planet Dwellers lived in space. Plus, she was just an orphan, alone in the world with her two dogs and her bike.

And yet here she was inside a ship as shiny as chrome, a ship from the galactic center, where they had technology far advanced of anything on Amatheon.

She still had her dogs with her. Big, black Gert was leaning against her right side, her head on Scout's thigh, but her warm eyes rolling up to look at Scout time and again to make sure everything was still okay. The smaller rat terrier Shadow was buckled against her left side, preferring to stand with his body rigid as he looked around. His name was a misnomer, his fur being mostly white with just a few black spots. But then her father had named him Shadow, not for his looks but for his behavior, as he always trailed after Scout wherever she went.

Yes, the dogs were still with her, but her bike was long gone. Not that she would need it now that she was heading into space. She had left it in the back of the rover—the rover she had crashed into a canyon wall while fleeing from the rebels. She was never going to see it again. She wasn't sad about that, exactly; it had been a good bike, but it hadn't been the bike her father had left her with. That bike she had loved, but she had outgrown it years ago.

She *was* a little sad about her father's hat. She wished she still had it as a remembrance of him. She wasn't sure where she had lost it. Probably also when she had crashed the rover. The bump on the head she had gotten in the crash made everything that had happened right after it a bit of a blur, and her second escape had happened so quickly it had really been a blur.

"Ready?"

Liam, the off-duty galactic marshal who'd come to get her to fulfill the wishes of his recently deceased partner, had been tapping away at a computer console set in the center of the panel in easy reach of both seats. Whatever he had been doing, he had finished now and was looking over at her, his question echoed in the arch of his ginger eyebrow. Scout tucked the dogs closer to her sides and made sure the restraints holding them to the chair were tight. Then she gave Liam a nod and watched as he flipped a switch.

The ship around them started to softly vibrate, and Scout fought the urge to shut her eyes. She was somewhere between very nervous and outright scared, but there was no way she was going to miss seeing any part of this journey.

She waited for the firing of the rockets, waited to be crushed back into the soft chair beneath her, waited for the rumbling roar of engines defeating gravity.

Then the heavy stalks of grain that had been partially blocking the view out the window shook and fell away and Scout realized the ship was already lifting up into the air. There was barely any sound, just that soft vibration. There was nothing crushing her into her seat, just a feeling like some giant's hand was gently lifting them up into the sky.

"Have we taken off?" Scout asked. Even leaning forward, she could see nothing but sky out of the window.

"Yes, would you like to see?" Without waiting for an answer, Liam touched something else on the control panel in front of him and the floor beneath her disappeared.

Scout yelped at the sight of her feet dangling hundreds of meters over the prairie. Then she realized the floor hadn't been breached; she was looking at a display screen that a moment before had been just another of the many chrome panels that made up Liam's ship. They all looked the same, only the size of their rectangular shapes varying, but each seemed to hide a secret function. One had folded out into a sink, another had become a computer capable of reading the encrypted data disks Scout had brought to him.

Scout pushed the thought of the disks and all she had been through on their account to the back of her mind. She was going into space, an amazing experience in itself, but she was also leaving her home world behind. She intended never to see it again. She wanted to give that beautiful landscape a proper farewell. Governments and rebellions and their web of secrets and lies would still be there to stew over helplessly later.

She could see the swirling, flattened pattern in the grass that marked where the ship had been. But they were rising higher now, high enough that she could see the edge of the prairie and the beginning of the hill country. The delicate bands of color that made the canyons so breathtaking when seen from the ground were just a uniform reddish brown from this distance. But the crags and breaks of the canyon walls that had been all around her the day before were no more than a fine tracery of lines from above, beautiful in their meticulous detail.

Scout thought she saw a plume of dust from a moving vehicle, perhaps one of the rebels still searching for her. But that was in her past now. Her future was light-years away from all that.

Scout felt the wide smile that spread across her face at that thought. Light-years away. It was real. It was really happening.

Liam was glancing over at her now and again when not too occupied with piloting his craft. They had met only moments before, but he had the grin of an uncle showing something amazing to his favorite niece, eager to see her delighted response.

"Cool?" he asked.

"Very cool," Scout said. She could see three different domed cities dotted across the landscape spread out beneath her. They looked so small.

"Will we be able to see the Space Farer stations when we go by?" Scout asked.

"From a distance," Liam said. "The point where we slip through the blockade is as far from the space stations as possible."

Scout nodded, but she didn't really understand. Liam had mentioned something about a blockade and friends who had helped him get past it to get to her. Scout guessed it was all political, and she barely understood the politics of the world she had spent her whole life on. Galactic politics would be a lot to take on now, after Scout's last few days.

Once they got somewhere warm and safe, after she'd had a shower and changed into some clean clothes, after a couple meals' worth of proper food and perhaps even a bottle of jolo or two, maybe then she could focus on learning the nuances of galactic politics. For now, it was enough that Liam understood it and was taking her to the life his former partner, Gertrude Bauer, had promised Scout.

The blue of the sky through the windscreen was fading away, like watching a puddle drain and evaporate. Beyond it was black—inky, bottomless black. Scout's fingers curled around the edges of her seat cushion. She felt like she was falling into that black just looking at it, but still she fought the urge to shut her eyes.

Then the first stars winked to life, and she was glad she had won that battle. She knew she wasn't any closer to them here than on the surface, not really, but they looked like she could reach out and touch them.

The vibration of the ship around them, barely noticeable before, settled down to almost nothing, and the feeling of being buoyed up by a giant's hand went away.

"We're floating!" Scout said, looking down at her feet still dangling over the floor display. The planet beneath her was all patches of blue water, golden prairie, and reddish-brown hills in long rows. But as beautiful as it was, she scarcely noticed it.

Her shoelaces were definitely floating.

"We're safely out of atmosphere now, so you can unbuckle from your seat if you like," Liam said. "We'll see how the dogs like it."

Scout grinned, then unclasped the restraints. Shadow's tense body sprang away from her almost at once, and he gave a startled yip as he sailed through the air into Liam's waiting arms.

Gert trembled against Scout's side and then whimpered as she, too, started to float away. Scout caught her, holding her tight as the two of them tumbled slowly down the length of the ship until they bumped up against the back wall.

"Is it always like this?" Scout asked, laughing as Gert tried to stand against the wall and only pushed herself out into the middle of the room. Scout caught her paw and pulled her back into a hug.

"The stations are under spin; that simulates gravity," Liam said. "The larger ships like the one that brought your ancestors here use the force of their acceleration and deceleration to mimic it. But little ships like this one don't have anything like that."

"How long will we be traveling in this ship?" Scout asked. Shadow had pushed away from Liam and was paddling his feet madly but ineffectually as he tried to reach her and Gert. Scout reached out an arm, waiting for him to float close enough for her to grasp.

"We have to get out of the planetary system before we can—" Liam began, but he was interrupted by a chiming notification sound. Liam turned back to his controls and spoke in a voice too low for her to hear.

Scout caught Shadow, his little body trembling from perhaps too much adventure, and hugged both of her dogs while she waited for Liam to tell her what was going on. He was silent for a moment, then spoke again, still too low for her to make out any words. Then he tapped something into the computer between the two seats.

"We have to make a quick stop," he said as he touched more buttons.

Scout bit her lip. His tone was casual, almost jaunty, but clearly fake. He was trying to keep her calm. "Nothing to worry about?" she asked.

"No, nothing to worry about," he said. "Just a little bureaucracy that has to be cleared up before we can go."

"I thought your friends took care of all that," Scout said. "You had a way to sneak past this, I thought."

"It sounds like we just got caught up in a routine sweep. Something about weeding out black marketers. And since we aren't black marketers, this should just take a moment."

"Are you sure?" Scout asked.

Liam turned in his seat to look directly at her and gave her a reassuring smile. "Absolutely. I have the appropriate papers, and they have no reason to detain us. They're just being thorough. I promise, we'll dock for a few moments to deal with this and then we'll be on our way."

Scout released her lip from between her teeth and attempted to return his smile, but she was certain her attempt to seem unbothered was even less convincing than his.

2

SCOUT WATCHED the planet Amatheon slowly rotating under her dangling feet, sucking on a bulb of cool water Liam had given her after helping get her and the dogs buckled back into the seat. It had a faintly metallic taste, but it was also slightly sweet. She was starting to feel a little less lightheaded. She had been pretty severely dehydrated before she had reached Liam's ship.

Liam would occasionally murmur words into his comm, but other than that, there was no sound but the soft hum of the ship, the occasional yawn from a dog, and a slight hiss of air moving through the vents. The planet was beautiful, but the swirls of clouds slowly twisting beneath her were almost hypnotic. She blinked her eyes sleepily and took another sip of water.

She scarcely needed hypnosis to make her sleepy. Not after the morning she'd had. She had escaped her captors and made it to her rendezvous with Liam on time, but it hadn't been easy. After the rebel who'd pursued her had tried to stop her by shooting her dogs with tranquilizers, she had been forced to carry them both for kilometers under the hot Amatheon sun. It had been exhausting.

After losing her hat, the only other protection from the burning sun had been her shirt, which would have been enough, only she had been forced to use it as a sling to carry Gert on her back. Her skin felt prickly all over and was turning a frightening shade of red. That on top of the still-tender spot on her chest where she had been hit with a rock days before, the lump over her eyebrow from the rover crash, and abrasions all around her hips from her escape through an almost-too-narrow tunnel made her body one big throbbing, aching, exhausted mass.

And the day was far from over.

She hadn't realized just how slow her sleepy blinks had become until a hulking mass beneath her startled her fully awake.

It was massive, truly massive, eclipsing her view of the planet below. But aside from its size and its long, cylindrical shape, she could make out no details. The planet behind it was shining so brightly, all she could see of the orbiting object was its outline.

"Is that the space station?" she asked.

"*Amatheon Orbiter 1*," Liam said to her. "Formerly the colony ship *Tajaki 47*. Your ancestors arrived on that ship."

"It's huge," Scout said, moving Gert's head on her thigh to one side so she could bend over. Not that that gave her a closer look, but she couldn't help herself.

"About the size of two of your domed cities on the surface," Liam told her. "Of course, it was much bigger before it shed all the components you used to construct all of your cities."

Scout's mind boggled. She preferred the wide-open prairies to the crowded streets of the domed cities. This, being inside a dense station hull rather than a transparent dome, was sure to be even more confining.

A sudden vision bloomed in her mind of her and her dogs losing Liam inside that thing. Of getting lost and wandering endless corridors, unable to find him again.

"Do you know where we're going?" Scout asked, trying to keep her nervousness out of her voice.

"We enter from the far end and fly up the center of the cylinder to the hangar area," he said.

"No, I meant, once we're inside," she said.

"Oh, no worries," he said with another smile meant to reassure her. "The bureaucracy will come to us. We'll never even have to leave the ship. Bureaucrats always prefer it that way. They're in control and able to easily keep track of you. We'll be out of here in a jiffy."

Scout hugged her dogs closer to her sides.

Liam guided the ship around in a slow, lazy curve as their momentum carried them past the end of the space station. When the curve ended, they were turned completely around, facing the station that had just passed beneath them. From this angle Scout could see that the cylinder was hollow in the middle, a little crescent of the planet visible through that hollow, dark sky and winking stars filling out the rest of the circle that was the heart of the station.

Details became clearer as Liam piloted the ship closer to the station. The interior wasn't a perfectly circular cutout. No, the surface of the inner curve of the cylindrical hull was visibly jagged. A few lights, not stars but man-made lights, became apparent.

They were nearly inside the structure before her brain finally put it together: the jagged outlines were buildings. Unimaginably tall buildings, dotted with lights, all converging toward the center. There were other ships around them, smaller and rounder than Liam's long, gleaming needle of a ship, some zipping between the buildings, a few traversing the open space in the center of the cylinder.

"This is amazing," Scout said, trying to look everywhere at once and failing.

Liam shot her a look of surprise. "Oh, you're not joking," he said. "Kid, wait until you see Galactic Central. This is all pretty low-tech stuff. It may be your biggest orbiting station, but in broader terms, it's just a tiny speck."

"I can't wait," Scout said, although she was suddenly grateful for this unanticipated stop. Whatever awaited her at the end of her journey, she could use as many steps as possible to get used to it all.

Liam guided his ship to the brightest collection of lights atop a tower that was not the tallest inside the station, but was longer and wider. The lights were blinding at first, but then the brightest of them pivoted away all at once and Scout could see the platform was dotted with ships. Most were the small, round ones that were apparently native to the station. They shared a design aesthetic with the rovers back on the planet's surface, vehicles built for practical durability in a harsh environment. A few were larger, more elongated, but still clearly built from the same tech and materials.

Liam set the ship down on the landing platform, and Scout heard a loud clang.

"Magnetic clamps," he told her as his fingers flew over his control panel. "Not really necessary since this station is under gravity-simulating spin, but protocol is protocol."

Scout nodded, letting the words wash over her. She had a million questions, but they could wait until she and Liam had resumed their journey.

"Do you need more water?" Liam asked as he undid his restraints.

"Can you fill a bowl for the dogs now that we have gravity?" Scout asked. "I tried giving them squirts from the bulb, but I'm not sure they liked it."

"Of course," Liam said, moving to the back of the ship and making the sink reappear from its compartment. "And I don't have anything specifically made for dogs to eat, but I bet I can find something to tempt them."

"That would be good," Scout said, releasing the buckles just as Liam set the bowl on the floor. The dogs raced to it, both gulping the water down from opposite ends of the little bowl without fighting for space. The tranquilizers must still be in their systems. But Scout wasn't about to complain that her dogs were too well behaved.

She looked up from the dogs to see Liam looking at her with deep concern.

"What?" she asked.

"You've really been through it, haven't you?" he asked.

She looked down at her blistering skin and the tattered remains of her cargo shorts barely holding together over her hips. "It looks worse than it feels," Scout said as Liam leaned forward, examining the lump on her forehead. "It will all heal."

"Yes," he said distractedly, turning to stare at all the chrome squares that formed the walls of the ship. "There's a medical kit in here somewhere…"

A soft beep from the console at the front of the ship distracted him from his search. "Here they come," Liam said, looking out the windscreen.

The nose of the ship was set slightly lower than the back end, allowing them to see the surface of the landing platform in front of them. Four figures dressed in black were approaching their ship at a brisk walk. At first, Scout thought they were wearing uniforms, but there was no symbol or insignia on any of them, and although all their clothing was black, the details of the tailoring differed between each of them. Scout couldn't tell if they were men or women. They all wore black caps pulled low over their faces and walked with their heads bent.

"They seem awfully furtive for officials," Scout said.

Liam frowned. "I was thinking the same thing. I'm sure it's nothing to do with us. Just part of the general political unrest. I'll go down and talk to them. You wait here with the dogs. Once we're underway again, I'll break out the food and find that medical kit."

"Okay," Scout said, resisting the urge to tell him to be careful. He was a galactic marshal; he knew how to handle himself. But she couldn't help noticing that, unlike Gertrude Bauer, the last galactic marshal she had spent time with, Liam wasn't carrying a gun or even wearing a belt loaded with handy tools.

Liam touched a spot on the wall, and just as he had made the sink appear out of nowhere, now he summoned the outlines of a door. The door rolled partway up, but he didn't wait for it to finish, just ducked under it and stepped down the still-lowering ramp. He must have touched a control on the other side because the ramp and door both reversed course, closing up again before Scout's eyes.

That was probably wise. The last thing they needed was a couple of loose dogs roaming the platform.

Scout got up and refilled the dogs' water bowl; then, not knowing what else to do, she went back to her seat. She wanted to see what was going on outside, but she wasn't sure she wanted the people outside to see her.

Bureaucracy meant documents: identity cards and permissions to travel, things like that. Scout had a chip in her wristbone that identified her in the domed cities. She supposed it would still work here; the

Space Farers had all the technology the Planet Dwellers had, and then some.

But she didn't have permission to be here in orbit. Not for herself, certainly not for her dogs.

Liam was probably being honest with the officials, but just in case he was fudging some facts, Scout decided it was safer to stay out of sight.

It might be safer, but it was maddening not knowing what was going on as the seconds ticked into minutes and the minutes began to accumulate.

Scout chewed at her lip, straining to hear through the hull of the ship. She was certain it was impossible for most sounds to travel through it. There might have been a soft murmur of voices, but Scout could never quite be sure, not with the dogs sniffing madly at every centimeter of the ship's interior, occasionally whuffing out sharp breaths when they located a particularly interesting scent.

Focusing on trying to hear the nearly inaudible was tiring. Her eyelids were getting heavy again.

She snapped awake, heart pounding. Her brain was in the foggy place of not being able to separate dream from reality, especially as she hadn't even realized she had been sleeping. But even if she hadn't just dreamt it, surely that softest of sounds she thought she had heard wasn't enough to warrant such a rush of adrenaline. She wasn't even certain what she had heard or if she had imagined it. She looked to the back of the ship. Had one of the dogs made that squeak?

But the dogs were both listening intently themselves, heads tipped and ears cocked crookedly.

Scout bit her lip. Had it been a yelp, abruptly cut off?

She needed to see outside, but she still didn't want to be seen. She leaned forward towards the windscreen, keeping her eyes level with the top of the control console. Someone might see the top of her head, but she had to risk it.

The landing platform was much busier than when they had landed. Two larger ships were sitting on either side of them now and people were disembarking. Most wore the gray jumpsuits of the Space Farers she had encountered down on Amatheon, but a few were decked out in suits of brighter colors.

Then she saw them. The four figures in black were hustling away from the ship, back the way they'd come. But there was now a fifth person between them. At first Scout thought this one was also all in black, but when the figure stumbled, she realized what she had taken as a hat was actually a black hood pulled down over their head to spill around their shoulders, covering the top of their khaki jumpsuit.

Scout's fingertips gripped the edge of the console so tightly they quickly went cold and white. They were taking Liam away. They had put a sack over his head and were dragging him away.

Whatever was going on, it was far more sinister than mere bureaucracy. And with Liam gone, Scout was left to face it alone.

3

SCOUT WANTED to bolt out of the ship and run after Liam so badly the muscles in her legs were twitching, but she gripped the console tighter and stayed where she was. The ship's door was so slow to open, the ramp so slow to descend, that even if she charged out as soon as the gap was large enough, she didn't think she'd be in time. The bodies around Liam were hustling him through the milling crowds too quickly. The people from the two larger ships were moving in all directions towards more than a dozen open gateways that led off the platform. If she ran out into that without knowing where they were going, she'd never find Liam.

And she couldn't take her dogs with her, not out into that chaos of strangers.

So she remained where she was, but she did stand fully up to keep her eyes on Liam's black hood. The hood and the four figures in black stood out starkly in the landing platform's bright lighting. She watched as they approached one of the smaller gateways. Scout cast her mind back and formed a mental picture of the landing platform and everything around it, as she had noticed it when they had been on their final descent. The platform hadn't extended to the edges of the tower; the gateways went into a narrow space that probably contained any number of elevators going down to the city below.

She thought the gateway they were going into corresponded to one of the narrow walkways that connected this tower to the taller tower next to it, but she wasn't sure. Even if it did, there were an infinite number of ways to go from there. Knowing which gateway they'd taken wasn't going to help much at all.

Then he was gone from sight, and she was alone with her dogs.

Scout looked at the people in the crowds. Had no one noticed a man in a hood being taken away against his will? Was this not even remotely unusual here?

But then everyone did seem to be aggressively minding their own business, hoisting bags up onto their shoulders as they stepped down ships' ramps, catching potentially wayward children by the hand and hurrying them to one of the gateways. Reflective lines painted on the platform marked out where it was safe to walk, but it didn't seem to take much to launch a ship off the platform and up into the weightless center of the station. If someone fired all their rockets for whatever reason, they could hurt a lot of people, but there didn't seem to be enough room to make things any safer.

A passing child made eye contact with her looking out the windscreen and pointed up at her, tugging at his mother's hand as he tried to get her attention. Scout dropped back into the passenger seat, slouching low. She doubted the kid could get her into trouble, but best not to risk it.

How long could she wait for Liam to return before she was certain he wasn't coming back?

What could she do besides wait?

Gert came up to her and put a paw on her thigh, her usual sign that she needed to go out. Shadow rushed up to sit beside her in his usual rigid stance of attention, but his quiver of anticipation gave him away. He needed to go out, too.

Scout sighed, but she got up and went to the back of the ship and started opening cabinets. She found a spool of thick, rubber-coated cord in one of them—not ideal, but workable. She searched a bit longer to see if she could find anything better, but there was no rope or string or anything. The cord looked like it was meant to connect electronic devices together. It was supple and thick enough to make a strong knot that she could still later untie when she needed to. It would work. She just hoped she wasn't ruining anything expensive or hard to replace.

Scout cut two lengths from the cord, then tied one to each of the dogs' collar. She kept the cords short so the dogs would have to stay close to her. They weren't wildly enthusiastic about being on makeshift leashes—back home in the prairies of Amatheon they roamed freely nearly all the time—but they sat quietly and let Scout do what she had to. Then she found the control to open the door and waited for it to roll up and the ramp to extend down, taking deep breaths and trying not to let the dogs sense how nervous she was about leaving the ship.

The air was cool but had an odd smell to it, almost electric, like just before a thunderstorm. The dogs sniffed the air anxiously but charged down the ramp the moment it touched ground, dragging Scout after them.

There was nowhere to go. No patch of grass or sand or anything. Not surprising, since they had landed on top of a tower. The dogs pulled her to one of the back landing legs. She had to duck to avoid hitting her head on the curving belly of the needlelike craft.

"Hey!" someone yelled. Scout jumped, then clutched the cords more tightly before looking around. A young man with more dark stubble on his jaw than on his shaved head was stalking towards her. The dogs saw him approaching. Shadow growled a warning while Gert tried ineffectually to hide behind Scout's legs. "You can't have them out here. They need to be in transport crates."

"Okay," Scout said. "I didn't know."

"That's no excuse," he said, but she could see his anger was dissipating. Now that he was close enough to get a good look at her, she could see he was appalled by how dirty she was and how battered and torn her clothes were. Well, she had had a tough last few days, squeezing through the tunnel that hadn't quite been large enough for her to fit through being one of the clothes-destroying highlights. His gaze stopped at the point just above her eyebrow where she had hit her head. She hadn't had a chance to take a look at it herself, but it must look worse than it felt, to judge by the concern on his face.

Maybe she could take advantage of his change of heart. "Can you help me? The man who brought me here was just dragged off by some people in black clothes."

"I'm ship's crew, not a platform worker," he said, his tone not as snappish as before, but still firm. "I need to get back to work."

"Where can I find a platform worker?" Scout asked.

"They'll find you," he said, with an ominous air. "But get the dogs off the platform."

"Yes, sir," Scout said, and pulled the reluctant dogs back up the ramp.

She hoped he was right and that someone would come and find her. But she didn't want to bet on it. She certainly didn't want to wait.

The dogs went back to their bowl but seemed disappointed to find it still contained only water. Food would have to wait. Scout took a deep breath, then slipped into Liam's pilot chair. She found the little earpiece he had left on top of the console and carefully fitted it over her ear.

"Hello?" she asked.

She could hear far too many voices all gabbing at once, but none of them responded to her. She looked around for the communications panel. She wasn't sure what any of the settings meant except for one: the one labeled EMERGENCY. She pressed that one. The chatter of voices instantly stopped, only to be replaced by a hiss of dead air.

"Hello?" she said again.

"This line is for emergencies only. Please disconnect," a woman's voice said to her curtly.

"But this is an emergency," Scout said. "My pilot has been kidnapped."

"You're on the wrong channel. Please disconnect," the voice said, downright testy now.

"I need help," Scout said, speaking slowly and clearly. "Please."

But the woman was gone. Scout listened to the warbling hiss of nothingness for several minutes before tossing the earpiece aside with disgust.

"Maybe we should go back outside," Scout said to the dogs. "If I get arrested for having dogs outside of a transport crate, at least someone will be listening to me then."

But she didn't like that option. In the cities, when kids her age were picked up for being out after curfew, they were put into detention centers. Kids with dogs were separated from them, and even when the kids were reunited with their parents, the dogs were never seen again. She didn't know if they did that up in space as well, but she didn't want to risk it.

Scout watched as the two larger ships loaded up with cargo and passengers, then took off, one after the other. The platform was quieter now. A few workers in gray jumpsuits were doing some sort of maintenance on one of the round ships, and a group of six travelers were chatting at the crossing of two walkways, but everything else was still.

Was it nighttime now? Or was it always this dark?

A flash of red caught her eye, and she saw a girl about her age in one of the ubiquitous gray jumpsuits walking out of one of the gateways. She walked quickly, dodging a spill of crates partially blocking the walkway, all without looking up from a tablet in her hands.

Scout felt another jolt of adrenaline. Too much. She hadn't fought or fled the last time, and this extra hit of unspent energy was making her hands shake.

That shade of red—bright, candy-colored red, not remotely a natural hair color—was familiar. The last time she had seen it, the girl with the candy-red hair had been very intent on killing her. She had nearly succeeded, too.

But this wasn't that girl. That girl had been younger, she had been on the planet surface with no means to get up into space, and besides all that, the girl had been murdered before Scout's eyes.

She doubted this shade of red necessarily meant girl-assassin, but her nervousness only increased when the girl on the platform headed straight to Liam's gleaming ship and pressed the call button.

The dogs, startled by the electronic chiming sound, both started barking like mad.

She could scarcely pretend to not be there. And this might be someone sent to help her.

Or to put a bag over her head and drag her away.

Scout looked around the ship, ignoring the second chime of the door. If she was about to be dragged out of here, what should she have with her? She dug under the pilot's seat and found the belt she had given to Liam just over an hour before. It had belonged to his former partner, and while the gun was long gone, the other devices attached to it could come in very handy. She buckled it around her waist, running a hand down the front of her shorts. The mirrorlike lens that let her interact with the belt's equipment was still there, scratched and missing the other half of the pair, but still workable.

The door chimed again and Scout headed to the control to lower the ramp, but she again delayed that action to open a different cabinet. This one hid a computer as well as the two data disks that had fallen into Scout's hands after their original spying owners had died. The data was all compromised now that the rebellion had copied it to their own computers, but information might still prove a useful thing to have.

Data disks hidden deep within the pockets of her frayed shorts, Scout at last grabbed both of the cord leashes and held the dogs close to her side before opening the door. The girl stayed where she was at the bottom of the ramp, eyes on the tablet, for another moment before looking up at Scout through a pair of glasses with chunky black frames.

"I need to download your flight data," she said.

"You're not here to help?" Scout asked.

The girl looked puzzled. "I'm here to help with the flight data."

"I don't know what that means," Scout said.

"I need your permission to come aboard."

"Okay, but it's not my ship," Scout said.

The girl seemed to consider that good enough, striding up the short ramp and brushing past Scout and the dogs to get to the front of the ship. The dogs sniffed at her as she passed and seemed to find her unobjectionable.

Her hair might be the same color as the girl assassin's, but on closer inspection, the style was very different. The assassin's hair had been short and stood straight up in aggressive spikes. This girl's hair was shaved at the backs and sides, but the pile of tight curls on top of her head was quite dense. It looked short from a distance, but Scout suspected if she pulled one of those curls out straight, it would be nearly as long as her own honey-blonde hair.

The dogs trusted her. That had always been enough for Scout in the past. She swallowed nervously, then tried redirecting the conversation again. "The man who owns this ship was just dragged off the platform with a bag over his head. Is that normal?"

"Normal for who?" the girl said, an emptiness to her tone that said her mind was focused elsewhere. She connected her tablet to the ship's computer and started tapping at buttons. Gert was whimpering against Scout's knee and Scout put a hand on her black head to calm her. Shadow was straining at the end of his leash, curious what the strange new girl was up to and wanting to explore her scent further.

Scout saw the patch on the shoulder of the girl's gray jumpsuit and recognized the Space Farer logo shaped like a rocket.

"Normal for Space Farers," Scout said.

The girl raised one dark blonde eyebrow higher than the top of her glasses. "Space Farers," she repeated.

"Yeah," Scout said.

The girl blinked. "You're not from around here," she said.

"I just landed here," Scout said. "In this ship, which doesn't look like any of the other ships." She knew her voice was edging towards sarcasm. That always happened when she was tired and annoyed. Of course, she wasn't a Space Farer. That was beyond obvious.

"This is a galactic ship. But you're from down there." The girl cocked a thumb over her shoulder in what Scout decided must be the general direction of the planet, although with the station constantly rotating, it surely wasn't an accurate gesture.

"How can you tell?" Scout asked.

The girl looked her over slowly and deliberately. She winced as her eyes moved over the lump above Scout's eyebrow but didn't ask about it, didn't even speak until her thorough assessment was complete. "Your skin is sun damaged, you're covered in some sort of red dirt, and you use the term 'Space Farer,'" she said.

"Isn't that what you are?" Scout asked.

"Only you 'Planet Dwellers' use that term," she said.

"What do you call yourselves, then?" Scout asked, mustering as much politeness as she could despite her rising annoyance.

"We call ourselves and you the same thing," the girl said, disconnecting her tablet from the computer and retracting the cable with a whiz and a click. "Crew of the colony ship *Tajaki 47*. That's what the patch means," she added, touching her own shoulder. "That's what we are."

"We were just at war," Scout said. "There were two sides. We're about to be at war again."

The girl made a minute adjustment to her glasses, then squatted down to hold her free hand out to the dogs. Shadow rushed to lick at her, Gert coming more slowly. The girl didn't once crack a smile as she scratched around each dog's ears. Scout couldn't get any sense of this girl, friend or foe, except that she seemed a bit odd.

But the dogs liked her.

The girl straightened back up, slowly wiping her palm down the side of her jumpsuit and glancing again at her tablet. "Mutiny," she said at last, and Scout had to cast her mind back to remember what they had been talking about. "It's a mutiny, not a war. I find it best to stay well out of it."

Scout nodded glumly. "If only that were possible," she said, mostly to herself.

"I know how you feel," the girl said, putting a hand on Scout's shoulder and giving it a squeeze. Like she was trying to lend comfort but didn't quite know how it was done. And yet there was something in those gray-green eyes behind the thick black-framed glasses that said to Scout this girl really did know how Scout felt.

They both knew what it felt like to be unable to stay out of the fray, to avoid being collateral damage. They both knew what it felt like to be powerless and unsafe and alone.

4

THE GIRL PULLED her hand from Scout's shoulder and refocused her attention on her tablet a moment before Scout heard the sounds of others approaching the bottom of the ramp. She made sure of her grip on the dogs' leashes before turning to see who was coming. She wasn't sure if she was hoping for more figures in black or for more gray jumpsuits like the girl was wearing.

The three people approaching wore neither. The blonde woman in front wore a navy-blue pair of slacks and a lighter blue tunic with navy-blue epaulets. A row of insignia was displayed over her right breast, and although none of them meant anything to Scout, the look as a whole said uniform. The young man on her left wore a jumpsuit of a deep forest green with a patch on his shoulder: the Space Farer rocket. The young woman on the right wore jeans and three shirts layered: a black turtleneck under a khaki button-up shirt with another thicker oversized flannel shirt pulled over everything like a sort of jacket.

Scout had another of those little jolts of realization. Here in space, there would be no weather to protect against. You wouldn't need a jacket to keep out the wind and rain or protect from the harsh light of the sun. All you had to worry about was warmth. She pulled the dirty, wrinkled folds of her sun-protective shirt closer around herself. She was pretty far from warm.

"Ensign… Tonnelier, is it?" the woman said as the threesome pulled up to a stop at the bottom of the ramp.

"Yes, sir," the redheaded girl said. "I was just collecting the navigation data."

"Were you sent here specifically?"

"No, sir. Just routine."

"I see. Well, if you've finished, you may go."

"Thank you, sir," Ensign Tonnelier said and slipped back down the ramp. She headed back the way she had come, eyes once more glued to her tablet.

Then another girl in a navy blue jumpsuit passed her on the walkway and Scout saw the ensign look up from her tablet. Ensign Tonnelier touched a hand to the temple of her glasses, giving them a tiny adjustment, but never slowed her steps.

Scout didn't know what it was about that gesture, but it seemed like a form of communication. If the girl in the navy blue jumpsuit understood it, she didn't acknowledge it. They might be the same age, but they didn't look like they would hang in the same social circles. This girl's long, dark hair was neatly braided and wrapped tightly around her head like a crown and her jumpsuit looked crisply new. Her eyes were lightly lined with kohl and small earrings glinted on her earlobes. Scout guessed this girl knew the uniform regulations backwards and forwards and followed them to the letter. She even walked with an air of maximizing the efficiency of each movement.

"Ensign Malini, you're late," the blonde woman said.

"Sorry, sir. I was copying what information we have on this ship," the girl in the navy blue jumpsuit said, handing the woman a tablet of a slimmer design than the one Ensign Tonnelier had been carrying. The woman glanced at it.

"Well, that's surely faked," she said.

"Yes, sir," Ensign Malini agreed, taking the tablet back and showing it to the woman in all the shirts.

"Why would a black marketer try landing here?" the woman in all the shirts asked.

"Why indeed," the blonde woman echoed, finally looking up the ramp to where Scout stood flanked by her dogs. She frowned, and Scout could just tell that when this woman frowned, people jumped to fix whatever was vexing her. "Are they dangerous?" she demanded.

Scout looked down at the dogs, Shadow guarding the top of the ramp diligently, but Gert once more cowering behind Scout's legs.

"No," she said. "Are you here about Liam?"

"Who's Liam?" the woman asked.

"Liam McGillicuddy. The pilot of this ship. He was abducted when we landed."

The woman turned to look at Ensign Malini, who shrugged. "This is news to me," the woman said to Scout.

"Then why are you here?" Scout asked, not quite a wail of despair.

"I'm here to ask you that very question," the woman said with a warning edge to her tone. "Why are *you* here?"

"We were told to land," Scout said. "Some bureaucratic thing."

"By whom?"

Scout felt her face flushing red. "I don't know. They spoke to Liam."

"This landing platform isn't even cleared for this sort of foreign traffic," the woman said.

"We didn't know," Scout said.

"And dogs can't be running loose here."

"They're not loose," Scout said, clutching the jury-rigged leashes.

"They should be in transport crates until you get to your destination," the woman said.

"Look, I'd love nothing more than to get out of your hair, but I can't fly this ship. You have to help me find Liam."

"Young lady, I don't *have* to do anything," the woman said, ratcheting up the warning in her tone to frightening levels.

"Please?" Scout asked.

The woman turned back to look at the others.

"I can check with security," the man said.

"Do that," she said, and he nodded and then jogged across the platform, not bothering to stick to the walkways defined by the reflective lines.

"We should crate those dogs," the woman in the flannel shirt said.

"Please don't," Scout said. "We won't come out of the ship."

"That might not be an option," the blonde woman said. She turned to the woman in flannel. "Captain Suze?"

"No, that's not an option," Captain Suze said. "There should be some spares in your veterinary processing area. You deal with this, if you don't mind, and I'll go see."

"Thank you, Captain," the blonde woman said. Suze nodded and walked off. Scout blinked hard. She didn't like where this was going.

Then the blonde woman was looking at her again like Scout, and her dogs were a most unwelcome snarl in her otherwise orderly day.

But her face softened as she came up the ramp, holding her hands out for the dogs to smell. Then she looked up at Scout and Scout saw the now-familiar wince response when the sergeant got her first good look at Scout.

"Has this Liam been hurting you?" she asked.

"No, this all happened before he rescued me," Scout said, touching her fingertips to the sore spot. "He was abducted before we could break the med kit out."

"You're going to need more than a med kit," the sergeant said, then sighed. Clearly, dealing with the pilotless ship and Scout and the dogs was still going to be a nuisance, but her annoyance was fading into grim acceptance. She looked up at Scout again. "You and I have to sit down and figure this out. Will your dogs behave?"

"Yes," Scout said, leading them to the front of the ship. She sat in the passenger seat. It felt appropriate to leave the pilot's chair for this woman with her air of command. The woman seemed to think so too, sliding into the chair and finding the controls to change its position to face Scout as if by instinct. Scout fumbled a bit, then found the buttons that would turn her seat to face this woman.

The woman brushed an invisible speck off the leg of her trousers before sitting forward, elbows on her knees and hands clasped. "First of all, I'm Sergeant Murray. I'm in charge of security for this landing platform."

"Scout Shannon."

"Where are you from, Scout?"

"Sunshine Valley."

That must have been the last thing the sergeant expected Scout to say. She sat back with a hiss of breath, and Scout watched as the shock on her face melted into an almost motherly concern. Then that morphed into a more professional sort of concern.

Scout understood that. Her hometown had been wiped out when she was twelve by a rock dropped from space. By the Space Farers, or whatever they wanted to call themselves. It wasn't the only city they destroyed that day. It wasn't even the biggest. But Scout was certain that everyone up in space knew the names of all of those cities, just like everyone down on the surface knew them. And if the one Space Farer she had met before this day had been anything to judge by, their mourning for the loss of life was just as deep, even if mixed with regret or an uneasy justification for the actions taken that day.

But Scout also reckoned having such an obvious motive for revenge would flag her in the eyes of Space Farer security. Certainly Sergeant Murray's eyes were assessing her in a different light now.

"I am sorry," the sergeant said at last.

"It was a long time ago," Scout said, and they both ignored the way her voice hitched at the words. She had lost her whole family that day: mother, father, and baby brother. Only she and Shadow, who had been out in the prairie on her bike, had survived. It had been a long time ago, and yet that loss never seemed to feel any more distant.

"This isn't a Tajaki ship," the sergeant said.

"You mean it's not a Planet Dweller ship?" Scout asked.

"We don't use that term here," Sergeant Murray said.

"So I've been told," Scout said.

"The ships that travel between the surface and the orbiting stations are all components from the original colony ship *Tajaki 47*. They share a rudimentary design that's nothing like this ship," Sergeant Murray explained.

"I get it," Scout said. "The other ships around here mostly look like the rovers the early explorers traveled in. I believe this ship is from Galactic Central."

"But you don't know for sure? Were you abducted?" The motherly concern was sneaking back into her eyes. Scout squirmed. She didn't know what she could safely say and what should stay secret. "Are you in trouble?"

"Only since we landed here," Scout said. "Four people dressed all in black met Liam when he came out of the ship, but then they put a bag over his head and dragged him away through that gateway over there. But I don't know where they took him or why or if he's coming back. If you could just find him and bring him back here, we'll happily leave."

"Why did they take him and not you?"

"I don't think they knew I was here," Scout said.

"So who is this man you were traveling with who manages to find trouble within minutes of landing on my normally trouble-free plat-form?" Sergeant Murray asked.

Scout looked down at her dogs and said nothing.

"Liam McGillicuddy, sir," Ensign Malini said, coming up the ramp and once more holding out the tablet for the sergeant to take and glance at. "Galactic marshal."

"Galactic marshal," the sergeant repeated, and another sequence of expressions washed over her face, the outward sign of a flow of thoughts that passed too quickly for Scout to get a sense of it. "On this side of the Tajaki barricade?"

"It explains the irregularities with the ship identification," Ensign Malini said.

"Yes," the sergeant agreed, "but it doesn't explain Scout here." Scout could feel those eyes on her again.

"He was just giving me a ride," Scout said. "As a favor to a friend."

"What friend?"

"Gertrude Bauer. Another galactic marshal. She died a few days ago," Scout said. Another painful memory. They had only known each other a few days, but in that short time, she had become something between a mentor and a hero to Scout. Scout had named her big black dog after the marshal, as they had both saved her life.

Sergeant Murray heaved a sigh. "This is going to be a bit of work to tease out," she said to the ensign.

"Yes, sir. I'll put in an order for dinner."

"Excellent," Sergeant Murray said, rubbing her hands together and getting to her feet.

"What's happening?" Scout asked.

"I'm afraid it's going to be a long night for all of us," the sergeant told her. "We'll have to scan your chip and confirm your identity, and then we'll have to negotiate your fate with your government, which is always a gargantuan headache of a task."

"My fate?" Scout repeated. Why did that sound so dire?

"In all likelihood, you'll be sent back down to the surface," Sergeant Murray said. "Back to your family; I'm sure they miss you."

"I don't have a family," Scout said. "Just my dogs, and they're here with me."

"The dogs are a complication," Sergeant Murray allowed with another frown.

Scout felt her face twisting into an ugly scowl, but she managed to bite back most of her anger. "What about Liam?" she demanded.

"We'll look for your friend," Sergeant Murray promised her. "But he's going to have a lot to answer for. You do know he's not even supposed to be here? Well, maybe you don't."

"I understand that," Scout said, a bit of an exaggeration. "But after you find him and he answers all of your questions, then can you just let us go?"

"I'm afraid not," Sergeant Murray said. "I just can't imagine him having any kind of answer that is going to be compelling enough for him not to leave here for Galactic Central in the custody of the marshal service he'll no longer be working for. I'm sorry."

She reached out to give Scout's shoulder a squeeze with more genuine feeling than Ensign Tonnelier, but Scout flinched away from her grasp.

After everything that had happened, everything she had done, she was going to end up right back where she had started—only this time without the bike that meant her livelihood. And with a far more jaded view of the universe she had almost been able to see.

5

SERGEANT MURRAY SPOKE to Ensign Malini at the top of the ramp, the two leaning close together and keeping their voices low.

Scout couldn't muster up the interest to try to follow what they were saying. Shadow, as always, sensed her mood and hopped up onto the seat to curl up in her lap, pawing at her hand until she turned it over and let him nestle his head in her open palm. Gert sniffed at him briefly, but when he didn't respond, she flopped down to cover Scout's feet.

Somehow, everything was going to work out, she told herself. Whether she ended up in Galactic Central, stuck here on the space station for the rest of her life, or exiled back to the surface, somehow she would find a way to be okay. So long as she had her dogs with her, she could handle anything.

"Scout, I have some things to take care of, including monitoring the search for your friend. We have surveillance video of him being taken; we'll be able to follow him on that to his current location. I'll be talking with you again soon. For now, if you need anything, just ask Ensign Malini here. She'll help in any way she can," Sergeant Murray said.

"Am I waiting here, then?" Scout asked.

"No," Sergeant Murray said, exchanging a glance with Ensign

Malini. The ensign leaned down to look across the platform, then straightened up, shaking her head. "Well, for the moment," the sergeant continued. "Once the transport crates arrive, we'll be bringing you and your dogs into the security building."

"Can't I just wait here?" Scout asked. "I'd prefer to."

"I'm afraid not. We have protocols. But don't worry. We have showers, clean clothes, food, and cots to rest on for you. Your dogs will have to stay contained, but they will be with you, I promise. You will all be quite safe with us."

"Okay," Scout said. She wasn't wildly enthusiastic about leaving the ship—what if Liam came back and needed to leave in a hurry?—but a hot shower sounded so much nicer than trying to bathe from the sink in the back of the ship.

And there was no denying she had a stink. Worse than her dogs.

Sergeant Murray gave her a tight smile, then exchanged nods with the ensign before descending the ramp. Scout watched out the windscreen as the sergeant half walked, half jogged across the landing platform.

"What time of day is it here?" Scout asked. She was pretty sure it was late afternoon on the part of the planet she had left behind, but it felt like the middle of the night out the windows of the ship, not just dark but empty. The maintenance crew had finished up their work, and once the sergeant was out of sight, there was nothing stirring out on the platform.

When the ensign didn't answer, Scout turned to look at her and found she was yet again the target of a slow, wound-inspecting perusal. But there was something more clinical and less compassionate in her face, as if the ensign was wondering not if all those injuries hurt but how Scout had gotten each. And there was just a touch of respect, as if she knew how Scout's head was even now dully throbbing, her body aching, and yet she wasn't complaining.

Then the ensign finally seemed to hear the question. "Midmorning," she said, glancing at the tablet still in her hands. "Just past ten."

Scout groaned and slumped lower in the padded seat. She needed a nap.

Ensign Malini suddenly tensed up. It reminded Scout of Shadow on high alert, every muscle tight and quivering. The dogs sensed the change in mood around them and both sat up, looking around with ears cocked.

"What is it?" Scout asked, almost at a whisper. She followed the ensign's gaze out the window to see three men and a woman in gray jumpsuits with black vests approaching the ship. "Trouble?"

"Nothing I can't handle. Just stay here and keep your dogs with you. This will just take a minute."

Scout wrapped the cords that were the dogs' leashes around her hand, shushing them gently when they started to growl. Gert fell silent, then flopped back down to resume her nap. Shadow's growl died off in a soft woof, but he remained standing, pressing his body up against Scout's chest.

"Officers," Ensign Malini said by way of greeting. Scout could just see her standing at the bottom of the ramp, her back to the ship, but could only see the shining boots of the other four. "You may stop there, if you please."

"Move aside..." one of the men said, voice trailing off. Then he added "Ensign" and Scout realized he had been checking her uniform for rank markings.

"I can't do that, sir," she said. "I have orders."

"I'm changing your orders, Ensign."

"I'm afraid that's not possible, sir."

Her voice was calm and in control, but from Scout's vantage point, she could see the two hands placed behind Ensign Malini's back as she stood at attention were clasping each other tightly. Was the ensign in over her head here?

"Do you see this, Ensign?" the man asked. Scout couldn't tell what he was referring to.

"Indeed, I do, Captain," Ensign Malini said. "But your rank is irrelevant. You don't have authority here."

"That ship contains one of my people, Ensign," the captain said. "Now step aside so I can retrieve him."

"It's a she, sir," Ensign Malini corrected him.

"He, she—whoever is in there is represented by my government and as a citizen is entitled to certain protections."

"As I understand it, that is a matter still under negotiation, sir. When an agreement is reached, I will be informed. As, I assume, will you. In the meantime, the passenger of this vessel is under our jurisdiction."

"She will be turned over to us. That's how this works."

"Yes, sir, I expect she will," Ensign Malini said. "But in the meantime, I do have my orders. Sir."

"This is ridiculous," the captain seethed. "Such a waste of time."

Ensign Malini didn't answer, just stood at rigid attention. Scout hugged Shadow closer to her as she leaned forward, hoping for a glimpse of the man's face. He sounded livid.

Scout slipped out of the chair to sit on the floor, then edged closer to the top of the ramp. Shadow growled—perhaps at the strangers outside, perhaps in annoyance at Scout moving him about—but Scout quieted him with a hand to the top of his head.

She still couldn't see the other three above the knees, but the captain had moved closer to tower over Ensign Malini, who might be a year or two older than Scout but was several centimeters shorter than Scout and far shorter than this captain. His face was flushed as he loomed over the ensign, hands in fists planted on his hips. He was leaning in to get right in her face and force her to look into his glaring eyes. Scout saw the ensign's hands twitch tighter together, but she kept her head high, acting for all the world like there was no one on the platform but her.

"I'll be back," he spat out, then backed away to rejoin the others.

Ensign Malini remained where she was until they were out of sight, then turned to walk back up the ramp. She was opening and closing her hands as if to stretch them out after intense exercise.

"Is that normal?" Scout asked.

"Lately, nothing is normal," Ensign Malini said. The voice that had held so steady when speaking to the captain was quavering now. In anger, not fear.

"Those were Planet Dwellers?" Scout guessed.

"Yes, from the Enclave," the ensign said. "He's not wrong—Captain Brenner, that is. You'll be seeing him again. But high command isn't going to release you until every protocol has been respected."

"Why?" Scout asked.

Ensign Malini seemed surprised at the question. "You do realize the fact that the people on the surface formed a government to represent them and make demands on the rest of us is technically mutiny, right?"

"There's that word again," Scout said, rubbing her forehead. Her hopes of waiting until later to deal with politics were clearly destined to be thwarted.

"That's how upper management sees it. And they don't like catering to the demands of mutineers. But you are holding our access to food and trade goods hostage."

"Not me. I want no part of it," Scout said with a sigh. "I was supposed to be leaving all this behind."

"I don't think that's even possible," Ensign Malini said with a frown. "There's a barricade. No one gets in or out of the planetary system."

"Why?" Scout asked.

Ensign Malini seemed to consider and then discard several responses before settling on "That's just the way it is."

"So your sergeant is right, that when you find Liam he's going to end up being arrested?" Scout asked.

"I don't know. But she's very seldom wrong about things."

Scout sighed again, dropping her chin to rest on the top of Shadow's head.

"Is it that bad, on the surface?" Ensign Malini asked, lowering her voice as if afraid of being overheard.

Scout was about to readily agree that it was when she looked down the ramp at the bright lights of the landing platform dispelling what must be the eternal darkness of the space station if it was truly midmorning here. What she was hoping to escape from was still preferable to living here in the cold and the dark, she was sure.

"The planet is beautiful," Scout said. "The prairie under the morning sun glows like fire, all rippling grass and rolling hills. I spent the last few days in a canyon I'd never seen before. It was like someone had painted it, tiny bands of a million colors more intricate and intense than any rainbow. It was one of the most awe-inspiring things I've ever seen." Despite the fact that she had almost died there.

"I've never seen a rainbow," Ensign Malini said. "I've been on space stations my entire life. I've seen images, but it's probably not the same."

"No, it isn't," Scout agreed. "The smell of the grass after a rain shower, one of the light ones that just barely soaks the soil—that's one of the best things in the world."

Ensign Malini smiled, tipping her head to one side as if trying to imagine it.

"Of course, it's not all great," Scout said. "It gets intolerably hot most of the year. And the coronal mass ejection events are coming more frequently lately and lasting longer than before. That's a lot of days to spend waiting underground for it to be safe to return to the surface."

"But don't you live under a protective dome?" Ensign Malini asked.

"Not since the day an enormous rock fell from space and destroyed the city that had been my home," Scout said.

"I'm sorry," Ensign Malini said. "It's good those days are past us."

"If they don't come again," Scout said.

Again, Ensign Malini looked like she considered and rejected several responses before asking, "How did you survive the destruction of your home?"

"I was out on the prairie on my bike delivering a package to another city," Scout said. "Shadow was with me. But my parents and my baby brother were all home when it hit."

Scout watched the ensign's face closely. She was too young to be personally responsible, but surely there was guilt enough to be shared among all Space Farers? But what momentarily clouded the ensign's eyes was something else, some more personal grief. But before Scout could say a thing, the ensign had blinked it away and turned her attention to the dogs.

"So his name is Shadow," Ensign Malini said, bending to touch the rat terrier's head. "And the other one?"

"Her name is Gert," Scout said, and Gert lifted her head sleepily to see if she was being summoned. "She adopted the two of us not too long ago."

"Gert," Ensign Malini said, holding out her arms until the dog got to her feet and padded over to get pets. An actual smile appeared on her face and pure delight danced in her eyes.

"Do you have dogs here?" Scout asked.

"Not really," Ensign Malini said. "The ones that came on the original freighter were stored as embryos and only decanted down on the surface to be work-dogs. Since then, we used to have some contact and even trade with the rest of the galaxy, but now that's mostly on the black market. A few people have smaller dogs. They're not technically banned, but they're very hard to acquire."

"Are my dogs safe here?" Scout asked.

"You'll all be perfectly safe inside the security building," Ensign Malini said. "And you won't have any reason to leave there." She straightened up, her no-nonsense demeanor returning.

Scout hoped the ensign was right. It would be nice to have a shower and some food and just wait for everything else to sort itself out. But somehow she didn't think that was going to happen, at least not in any way she was going to like.

Especially if she was going to end up being handed over to the likes of that irate Captain Brenner.

6

CAPTAIN SUZE RETURNED with two transport crates sitting side by side on some sort of floating cart. Scout was torn between the urge to remain unseen and the urge to get a closer look at that cart. How could it float like that, and without making a sound?

Captain Suze stopped at the bottom of the ramp and hoisted the first of the two crates. They were quite roomy, either one large enough to comfortably hold both dogs together. There were lots of openings for ventilation or to let the animal inside look out at the world. Ensign Malini came halfway down the ramp to take the crate from Captain Suze, then passed it up to Scout.

"I have a few other fires to put out, if you can take this from here?" Captain Suze said to Ensign Malini.

"Yes, sir," the ensign promised her, taking the second crate. Captain Suze left the cart parked at the bottom of the ramp and jogged off.

"Okay, dogs," Ensign Malini said, setting the second crate on the floor and opening the door on one side. "Time to get in."

"They might be happier about it if they can travel together," Scout said as both dogs recoiled at the idea of getting inside a box.

Ensign Malini thought for a moment, but in the end she shook her head. "Sorry, but we should stick with protocols. It might make things move smoother further on, when things get complicated, if we can demonstrate we followed every regulation to the letter."

"Okay," Scout said, not understanding much beyond the fact that she was going to have to separate the two dogs.

They didn't like it, and the cords still tied to their collars got tangled around everything as the two of them attempted to flee. Scout and Ensign Malini had to hop from foot to foot to avoid being tripped. Shadow tried running around the pilot's seat but was pulled up short when his cord got wrapped too tightly around a control stick protruding from the floor between the seat and the ship's hull.

Gert nearly made it down the ramp to freedom. Scout lunged after her, flinging herself headlong down the ramp but just managing to get a grip before the end of the cord could slip out of her hands.

Scout got back to her feet without losing hold of the leash, but Gert refused to go back up the ramp. Scout had to go down to where the big black dog had flopped bonelessly and scoop Gert up into her arms. She wasn't a light dog.

Scout finally stuffed Gert into one of the crates and Ensign Malini closed the door. The click of the latch falling into place made both dogs whine pathetically.

"I'm guessing this is a new experience for them?" Ensign Malini said, brushing a few loose hairs back from her forehead.

"We spend most of our time out on the prairie where they have complete freedom," Scout said, waiting for Shadow to calm a little so she could trace his cord back and figure out how to untangle him. "Even the leashes are a rarity for them."

"It seems almost cruel, bringing them here," the ensign said, "after having a whole planet to run around on. They are always going to feel confined here. We don't have any wide open spaces."

"We aren't staying here," Scout said, pulling Shadow up into her arms and yanking the cord away from the control stick.

But she didn't really know what life was going to be like wherever they were going. She had always pictured another planet with fields and hills and endless roads to travel along. But what if that wasn't where she was going? What if it was another space station with rules like this one?

She had been so eager to leave Amatheon she had never asked Liam even the most basic of questions.

She put Shadow inside the other crate and closed the door with a click. Then Ensign Malini hoisted one and Scout the other to carry them down the ramp to the waiting cart. The cart sank a few centimeters at first, then floated back up to its original height after adjusting to the change in weight. Scout found the controls to close the ship's door and retract the ramp, then poked her fingers through the holes in the crates. The dogs snuffled at her fingertips. Her scent calmed them a bit.

"Shall we?" Ensign Malini asked.

"Ready," Scout said. That crushing feeling of weariness was wrapping around her again, but it fell away as she took her first steps out from under the ship.

Looking out the windscreen and later standing just under the ship with the dogs had only given her a taste of the world around her: a small slice of landing platform, a glimpse of the gateways that swallowed up and regurgitated streams of people in intervals, a few winking lights from adjoining towers. Now that she was out of the ship, she could see more. And after a few steps, not even the ship was blocking her view.

Ensign Malini, towing the cart as she led the way, realized after several meters that Scout was no longer walking behind her and doubled back to where Scout was standing frozen, head thrown back as her eyes devoured the immensity of the space around her.

It was not remotely like being inside one of the domed cities. Even in the largest plazas, buildings crowded close around her, blocking her gaze from traveling far in any direction. Here, she could see everything: row after row of towers like jagged teeth, jutting in towards the center of the rolling cylinder that was the station. Scout could start in any direction and follow lines with her eyes until they wrapped entirely around and joined their own beginnings.

And yet the opposite side of the station, as clearly as she could see it, was still so very far away. Scores of ships drifted freely in the open space between, far from the highest peaks of any of the towers.

Scout looked directly above her. There was another patch of lights marking another landing platform right across from where she stood.

She felt like she could jump and float and land on that platform. Her mind kept trying to grasp the scale of things, making everything tiny and close one minute, then vastly huge the next.

In short, her head was spinning.

"You'll get used to it," Ensign Malini said. "Security is just through that gateway there. Let's go."

It was only when Shadow gave a yip that Scout came out of her vertiginous trance and followed after the ensign.

The landing platform was enclosed on all four sides by a low building, more open gateways than wall at the ground level. She could see windows dotting the second level, but the glass there reflected back the platform lights and gave no hint as to what lurked within.

The interior of the building was one continuous open ring, albeit squared off to enclose the landing platform. The inside wall facing the platform was more gateway than wall, and every gateway led out onto the same platform, although the colored lines on the floor were different from gateway to gateway. Scout supposed they marked out paths to different parts of the platform. They might serve a function when it was crowded, but they were less useful now when so few people were about.

Each gateway with its color-coded lines was opposite an obvious choice of direction on the other side of the ring, an opening either to a walkway or to the top of an escalator or bank of elevators. But there was nothing anywhere to indicate what the colors meant or what destinations they were guiding travelers to.

Ensign Malini led Scout to an unmarked door that opened to her raised palm. The hallway beyond the door was narrow and ended in a ramp leading up. Ensign Malini pulled the floating cart behind her, guiding it deftly around a narrow landing where one ramp ended and another continued up in the opposite direction.

Then they were in a large room with benches under long, narrow windows and chairs grouped around tables. There was no one there, and Scout had that same feeling of being up in the middle of the night.

Where was everybody? Or was it always like this?

"The barricade has cut down on the number of visitors we get these days," Ensign Malini said, as if reading Scout's mind. "I'm going to see if the vet techs are ready for you. I'll only be a moment. Please keep the dogs in the crates."

"Yes, of course," Scout murmured.

Ensign Malini disappeared down another hallway, and Scout was all alone with her dogs. She poked her fingers through the openings in the crates again, letting them sniff at her. Gert was whining low in her throat and Shadow was shaking all over.

"I'm sorry, you guys," Scout said, bending to press her forehead to the cold metal of the top of Shadow's crate. "This will all be over soon. I hope."

Gert flopped down inside her crate, burying her nose under one paw, looking around dolefully with her big, brown eyes. Shadow, being Shadow, preferred to remain standing at quivering attention.

Scout stepped away from the crates to look out the long row of windows. She saw the bright gleam of Liam's ship, so different from all the others. There was a rush of warmth in her chest at the sight of it there waiting for her to return. Scout almost laughed at herself. Less than half a day aboard that vessel and already she was thinking of it as if it were her home.

It might not be her home, but it was the only way she was getting out of this place. Either way, it meant a tremendous amount to her. The starbursts along its chrome-like hull where it reflected the landing lights banking around it. Surely that whiteness, almost too bright to be looked directly at, was what hope looked like.

"Scout Shannon? Hello. We're ready for the dogs now," a voice said behind her, and Scout turned to see that Ensign Malini had returned with two young women, all three in purple jumpsuits.

Scout frowned. Why had the ensign changed clothes?

"Okay," Scout said, starting to step forward, but Ensign Malini held up her hands.

"Oh no, you can wait here. It's easier for the techs to handle this on their own," she said.

"That's not what you said before," Scout said. "You said the dogs and I could stay together."

"And so you can, inside of this building," Ensign Malini said. "There is absolutely nothing to be alarmed about. But the techs need to do some exams and run some tests to be sure they're both healthy, and we need to do the same for you. It's more efficient if we do that all at once. You can trust me."

Scout bit her lip. She did trust Ensign Malini. After standing unbothered under pressure from Captain Brenner, there was no way she would cave under pressure from other ensigns in her own department. Sergeant Murray promised they would be safe, and Ensign Malini would see that they were.

And yet something felt off. Scout stepped closer, looking at the insignia on Ensign Malini's uniform. Everything was the same except the color of the jumpsuit.

"I have your word?" Scout asked. "This is the last time you change what I agreed to?"

"Of course," Ensign Malini said with a smile. She was more relaxed here than she'd been out on the landing platform. Perhaps her uniform had changed because of a change in her assigned duty?

"I don't know if I can trust you," Scout said. Ensign Malini was just smiling at her, hands clasped together in front of her while she waited for Scout to give her assent.

"Look at the dears," one of the techs said to the other, and they both leaned in to peek inside the crates. The dogs inside clawed anxiously to get out and say hello. They seemed to trust these new people well enough.

"They can roam free inside the veterinary processing area," Ensign Malini told her. "It will be good for them. And you'll all be back together as soon as your exams are done."

Short of making a huge dramatic scene—or breaking out her slingshot and making an even bigger, more violent scene—she didn't have any options to keep the dogs with her.

And she was worried that the tranquilizers the dogs had been hit with that morning might still be harmful. Aside from their attempted flight in face of the terror of being crated, they had been strangely lethargic since leaving Amatheon. If the techs could tell her for sure, it would be worth it.

Ensign Malini smiled again and turned to speak to the two techs. Then they towed the cart away, opening a palm lock and letting themselves into a room filled with glass-fronted cabinets and cold metal examining tables.

Scout felt a moment's rising panic, a sudden urge to throw herself through that doorway before the door could close and lock between her and her dogs. She curled her hands into fists and forced herself to be still.

Then the door clicked shut, and she was alone with the smiling Ensign Malini.

7

ENSIGN MALINI WAS STILL SMILING at her expectantly. Scout noticed that the tight braid the ensign had worn wrapped around her head like a crown when they were on the ship was loose now, not just untethered and left to drape forward over one shoulder, but actually braided looser. Some of the shorter hairs had sprung free when they had wrestled the dogs into the crates, Scout remembered. Had she redone her entire hairdo when she had changed her clothes?

"Is everything alright?" Ensign Malini asked, and Scout realized she was scowling.

"You look different," Scout said.

Ensign Malini's brows drew together in confusion, but then sudden dawning lit up her features. "Oh, I see. My sister Geeta must be on platform duty. I'm Seeta. Seeta Malini. Geeta and I are twins."

"Oh," Scout said. She had decided to trust one sister. Did that extend to this other?

"I'm sorry for the confusion. I didn't realize you had met her. I hope you don't think I was playing some sort of trick on you."

"No," Scout said. "I'm sorry. It's been a long day."

"Maybe more than just a long day," the new Ensign Malini said, her eyes on the lump over Scout's eye. "We should get you cleaned up before you go into the medical pod. But perhaps you'd like to check in with your dogs first?"

"I can do that?" Scout asked.

"You can't go into the veterinary processing area, but I can let you see them from the hallway. Come."

Scout followed her down a hallway. A row of windows on one side let anyone who might be in the hallway look inside the room without passing through the security doors. The two techs had let the dogs out of their crates and were letting them explore their new space while the techs hovered over an egg-shaped machine, the top half clear plastic, the bottom half made up like a bed without covers.

"They were so excited when we heard there were dogs here," Seeta said to Scout, her eyes on the activity in the room. "Working landing platform security, they mostly examine vat meat that passes through on trade vessels, not even real animals. They are fully trained, you have no reason to worry. But look at how happy they are."

One of the techs was lifting Shadow up in her arms to tuck him into the egg. The other had sprawled out on the floor to tussle with Gert, whose tail was wagging so hard her entire back end was a wiggling blur.

Scout didn't know if Seeta meant the techs or the dogs, but whichever it was, everyone inside that room looked happy.

"The machine runs a series of scans," Seeta explained as the tech closed the clear cover over Shadow. "But they both look healthy; I wouldn't worry. I'm sure if anything, they might have some diet deficiencies, and then that machine over there will calibrate appropriate food for each of them. By the time you are all ready to leave, they'll be in tip-top shape."

Scout mustered up a weak smile. She wanted to trust what was going on, but the nagging worry wouldn't stop running through her mind. Plus, she was exhausted. She never trusted decisions she made when she was this exhausted.

Setae's smile turned to a look of concern.

"I'm sure they'll be fine," Scout said quickly.

"Yes, but let's take care of you," Seeta said, grasping Scout's hand to lead her further down the hall.

"Why all the special attention?" Scout asked.

"Special?" Seeta repeated, the crease back between her brows. "This isn't special. You're only getting the attention any of us are entitled to as members of the colony. Perhaps you'll understand better after you've been here a bit."

"But I don't plan to stay," Scout said.

"That's a shame," Seeta said. "I know a lot of people who'd love to meet your dogs."

"Someone is watching the ship, right?" Scout said, looking back over her shoulder toward the waiting room. "If Liam gets back on his own and I'm not there—"

"No one is going to let him leave without you," Seeta promised her. "And if he escapes from the sort of people you described to the sergeant, he'll likely be right in here with you getting medical attention. Please don't worry. I know planetside you are exposed to all sorts of frightening propaganda about things up in space, but I promise we're all quite nice, really. We just want to make sure you are healthy and happy and cared for."

Scout bit back a sarcastic rejoinder that touched on quite nice folks dropping rocks on her entire family, along with thousands of other families. She was tired, getting cranky, and she really didn't need to start a political argument. Besides, the Malini twins were only a few years older than she was. They would have been maybe fourteen when the war ended, the war that started before any of them were born. The whys and wherefores were things they could only know secondhand, and who knew how much of what was passed down could be trusted.

Although, frankly, Scout knew propaganda had flowed in both directions. Maybe nobody knew what was true anymore.

"Here we are," Seeta said, turning into an open doorway. Scout found that lack of door reassuring; she wasn't about to be locked in anywhere. "You can leave your clothes on the bench here and shower just in there. Towels on that rack in the corner. I'll get you a gown to put on when you come out. The medical pods can be picky about some fabrics."

"Okay," Scout agreed, who didn't care if the rags that she was currently wearing ever touched her skin again. But… "My things?"

"You can put them in this bin for now," Seeta said, opening a locker and taking out a clear plastic tote. "You'll have to leave them on a shelf in the examining room while you're in the pod, but they'll stay in the same room with you."

"Okay," Scout said. That would have to be good enough.

"I'll be near. If you need anything, just give a shout."

Then, with one final smile, Seeta backed out of the locker room. Perhaps to wait in the hall; Scout didn't much care. She emptied her pockets, dumping lens and data disks, plastic dog whistle, slingshot, and stones all into the tote. Then she unbuckled the belt and draped it over the top. She stripped out of her clothes and left them in a pile on the floor, then stepped into the shower. She looked over the controls. They were identical to the ones she had found in the underground compound she had sheltered in during the last coronal mass ejection.

She spun a knob and deliciously hot water cascaded over her. The water that ran off her body to spiral down the drain was reddish brown at first—her skin had been packing more canyon dirt than she had realized—but soon it was running clear. The heat and intensity of the droplets pounding down on her had her muscles loosening deliciously, relieving cramps she hadn't even realized she had.

She found the soap, nothing fancy, but when she was done scrubbing and rinsing, she smelled infinitely cleaner.

Finally, reluctantly, she shut off the water and reached for the rack of towels. She wanted a brisk toweling-off that would leave her now-clean skin tingling, but her injuries objected to more than the lightest of touches. With the dirt gone, the long scratches over her hips and thighs stood out prominently, not just an angry shade of red but swollen as if she had tousled with a large, bad-tempered cat.

Seeta must have poked back into the locker room at some point, as a blue cotton gown was waiting for her next to the tote of her belongings and the clothing she had left piled up on the floor was gone. Scout slipped the gown over her head. It fell to mid thigh, the neckline high enough to cover the dark bruise on her chest. Once more, only her head injury was visible, although she couldn't see it herself. She touched the lump, trying to gauge the size.

"Ready?" Seeta called from the hallway.

"Yes," Scout said, picking up the tote.

"You look better already," Seeta said when Scout stepped out into the hall.

The floor was cold under her bare feet and she curled up her toes.

"Medical is just through here," Seeta said. "It's warmer in the pod, I promise."

While the dogs had gone into a pod shaped like an egg, the machine that waited in the medical bay looked more like a coffin, albeit a coffin with a little window over where her face would be. Seeta took the tote from Scout's hands and set it up on a shelf near the door, then lifted the coffin lid.

"Claustrophobic?" Seeta asked when Scout hesitated. Scout almost laughed out loud. What would a claustrophobic person have done in Scout's place the day before, when her hips had gotten wedged in a ventilation shaft deep under the canyon floor? Trapped in the dark with all that rock between her and the open air?

"No, I'm not claustrophobic," Scout said.

Seeta smiled again and held out a hand to help Scout get up on the bed inside the pod and lay flat. "Don't cross your arms or legs if you can help it," she said.

"If I can help it?"

"Some people fall asleep in here," Seeta explained. "It will be warm and cozy in a minute; you'll see." She started to close the lid, but then lifted it back up. "Did you want those clothes back? I can have them cleaned for you in a jiffy, but they are in a pretty bad state."

Scout didn't know what to say. The gown was soft enough, but she would freeze if that was her only other option.

"I can get you something else," Seeta said, again reading her mind. "Something warmer for when you're done here."

"That would be lovely," Scout said.

Seeta smiled again and shut the lid.

Warm and cozy indeed. Scout fell asleep almost at once. She dozed, vaguely aware of a series of hums changing in frequency, lights dancing over her, a nozzle blowing air across her face from time to time. The air smelled medicinal, but it was nothing so pungent as to pull her out of her nap.

Then all the sounds stopped and her eyes fluttered open. The lid was still closed, but she could see the room, even the tote of her things up on the shelf near the door.

She felt tingly all over. She reached up somewhat awkwardly in the small space and touched her forehead. The lump was gone; it wasn't even tender anymore.

Seeta's face appeared through the little window and then there was a click and the lid opened. "Feel better?"

"My fingers are all tingly," Scout said as Seeta helped her sit up.

"That's the nanites," Seeta said.

"I have nanites now?" Scout asked. The galactic marshal who had saved her life in that underground compound had had nanites. Among other body modifications, Scout suspected.

"Just the short-lived kind," Seeta said. "They are highly targeted. The tingling will go away when they've finished their work. If it tingles all over, you might have had some sort of infection."

"Are you a doctor or nurse or something?" Scout asked.

"Oh no," Seeta said with a little laugh. "I just help people like you navigate through the protocols. For instance, I've brought you some warmer clothes. Nothing too fancy, just what we wear in the morning when we do physical training before our shifts start. And double-thickness socks with slip-proof bottoms. These are great."

"Then what?" Scout asked, taking the little pile of clothing. It must have just come from the laundry. It was all so deliciously warm.

"Then I'll take you back to the waiting area for now. Sergeant Murray is with upper management, discussing your situation with the brass from the Enclave."

"What's the Enclave?" Scout asked.

"It's the tower we have set aside for the special use of the... Planet Dwellers?" She screwed up her face as she said the words, as if she wasn't sure she had the terminology correct.

"So, Captain Brenner?" Scout asked, her heart sinking.

"I'm not sure who they're talking to," Seeta admitted. "And I don't know a Captain Brenner, but maybe. In the meantime, the cafeteria is putting together a meal for you."

"And my dogs?" Scout asked, although her growling stomach attempted to talk over her.

"Well, about the dogs," Seeta said with a little frown.

"They're okay?" Scout demanded.

"They'll be fine," Seeta said. "They had something odd in their bloodstream, both of them."

"One of the rebels hit them with tranquilizer darts this morning," Scout said. "They woke up alright at about noon, but they were still lethargic after."

"Rebels?" Seeta said, but she shook her head, dismissing the thought. "It's okay. They just had to put them both in a light sedation while the countering agent does its work. So they're napping, but they'll be up and with you before the negotiations are complete, I'm sure."

"Okay," Scout said. Seeta left her alone to change.

Scout's hands were shaking as she pulled on the soft navy-blue shirt and pants, but not from the nanites and not from exhaustion or hunger.

No, her hands were shaking from pure rage. That rebel, Tucker, who had hoped to be more than a friend to her before he had betrayed her, had shot her dogs. And clearly he'd had no idea what the long-term effects of that would be on her dogs since he had been so focused on pleading with her to stay. She was glad she had nailed him with that rock.

He was nearly as lucky that her dogs were going to be okay as he was that she had only *almost* killed him with that rock. If Liam never returned and Scout was turned over to Captain Brenner to be sent back down to the surface, hunting Tucker down to make him pay again might be the only thing she'd have left to live for.

Wherever he was now, Tucker had better be wishing with all his might that all of this mess sorted itself out. If he knew what was in her heart, he would be the only person in the galaxy that wanted Scout safely in Galactic Central more than she did.

8

THE MINUTE they were back inside the large, empty waiting area, Scout went straight to the window to look out at the landing platform. Liam's ship was still there, still reflecting light in bright bursts all down its length. She hugged the tote containing her belongings—such as they were, only the slingshot and dog whistle being truly hers—closer to her chest as she gazed out at the platform. Another ship had landed, discharging streams of people to all the gateways. A trio of the round, rover-like ships was landing in a tight formation closer to Liam's ship, touching down almost delicately.

"Your food is ready," Seeta said, and Scout turned to see her lifting an insulating dome off the top of a place setting. Steam curled up from the bowl in a wispy twist so delicately perfect it looked like it came from an illustrated advertisement for comforting food.

"What is it?" Scout asked as she gave the ship one last wistful look before drawing closer to the lure of the food.

"Chicken and vegetable stew, bread and cheese, and some sort of juice, maybe a berry blend," Seeta said, given the glass a sniff and then nodding. "The medical pod measured some vitamin deficiencies in your body, so the cafeteria whipped this up to fill in some gaps in your diet."

"It smells good," Scout said, setting down the tote and sliding into the chair before the food. She leaned over the soup bowl and inhaled roast chicken and potatoes.

"I hope you like it," Seeta said, the dome still in her hands. "I'm going to leave you here alone for a bit, if that's alright. I have some things to check up on. When you're done eating, you can peek in on your dogs through the window I showed you. Or you can walk through the halls if you like. Just don't disturb anyone who's working, and don't try to go through any doors."

"Sounds good," Scout said, poking a spoon into the thick stew. The broth was more like a gravy, clinging thickly to the chunks of chicken and potato. There were green vegetables in there too, and something orange. Vegetables beyond potatoes were hard to come by on the parts of the planet where Scout roamed. She knew they had more variety further north, where the climate was wetter and milder. She wondered briefly where this food came from, then put the spoonful in her mouth and no longer cared.

Seeta smiled at the expression on Scout's face as she dug in for a second bite, then gave a little nod and left the room.

What had looked like a lot of food when Scout sat down was gone all too quickly. She had saved the thin slices of cheese for last, three of different intensities of orange. She took them with her and nibbled at the medium-orange slice as she walked back down the hallway to the window that looked into the veterinary processing area.

At first she couldn't see her dogs, but before panic could properly set in, one of the techs saw her looking in and pointed to what she had taken to be a wall of cabinets. It was actually a wall of kennels, and at the touch of the tech's hand, windows that had been opaque presumably to keep out the bright light became transparent. Both dogs were deeply sleeping, Shadow curled up with one paw reversed to support his chin, Gert flopped over on her back with her paws in the air. The paws twitched ever so slightly as she dreamed. Scout took that as a good sign and smiled her thanks to the tech.

In the next room over, she could see more vet techs extracting samples from the tops of large metallic cylinders and putting the samples into some sort of machine. Scout wondered if they were checking the vat meat, like Seeta said. Scout had eaten vat meat her entire life, but she'd never actually seen a vat before. Was the entire thing filled with meat, or was the meat floating in some sort of solution?

Scout decided she really didn't want to know and stepped away from the window.

She walked further down the hall, nibbling at the second, sharper slice of cheese. No one was in any of the hallways, but every window she stopped at looked into another room full of busy workers in brightly colored jumpsuits, sorting through crates or interviewing groups of travelers.

Eventually, the hallway led back around to the still-empty waiting area and Scout went back to the window overlooking the platform.

The ship was still there. She wondered how much longer she'd have to wait.

She sat on the bench with her back to a support pillar so she could keep looking out the window while she ate the last slice of cheese. Despite the soft warmth of the clothing Seeta had given her, Scout still felt cold. She pulled her hands back into the ends of the sleeves and tucked them into her armpits and drew her knees up tighter against her chest.

She wished she had a hat. Maybe not her father's bush hat—no need to shade her eyes here in this sunless place—but something knit for warmth would be nice.

She didn't realize she had dozed off until she snapped awake at a hand gently touching her shoulder. She sat up, stretching her hands back out of the sleeves, and looked up at Ensign Malini. Which one?

Navy blue—that meant Geeta. Also, the lack of cheery smile was a bit of a giveaway. But not only was Geeta not smiling, she looked downright grim.

"Is it the dogs?" Scout asked.

"Sergeant Murray wants to talk to you," she said.

"Okay," Scout said, looking past Geeta. Although someone had come while she had been napping and cleared the dishes from her meal away, there was no sign of Sergeant Murray.

"In her office," Geeta clarified. "This way."

"Not good news?" Scout guessed as she got to her feet.

"We still have options," Geeta said, pressing her palm on the lock next to a door. It opened with a click and she stepped aside to let Scout go through first.

"Options?" Scout repeated.

"I'll let the sergeant explain," Geeta said. But she added, so low Scout could scarcely hear her or even see her lips move, "Remember you have friends."

That was an odd thing to say. Scout had never really had friends. Was it some kind of Space Farer code?

Geeta opened another locked door and Scout found herself in a tiny office with no windows. The space was dominated by a large desk; Sergeant Murray, sitting on the far side, would have to turn sideways to squeeze her way past it to get to her chair. Geeta nodded at a stainless-steel chair facing the desk and Scout sat down on the edge of it.

It was cold.

"Scout Shannon," Sergeant Murray said, as if needing to call up the details of Scout's case in her memory. "I trust you've been well cared for during your time with us."

"Yes," Scout said. "Is that time over?"

"Nearly," Sergeant Murray said. "We will be bringing you to the Enclave in just a moment and turning you over to the care of Captain Brenner."

"I can't refuse to go?" Scout asked.

"I'm afraid not. This is a politically fraught situation. You've become the latest pawn in that game. There is nothing any of us can do about that."

Scout looked up at Geeta, who was standing near the doorway at attention, her face carefully blank as if she heard nothing going on around her.

"There must be someone I can appeal to," Scout said.

"Indeed, there is, but you will need to take care of that from within the Enclave," Sergeant Murray said. "The officers in charge there are the ones controlling your fate."

"But what about Liam?" Scout asked.

"We are still searching for him," Sergeant Murray said. "We

followed his trail on surveillance footage down to the base of the tower into the space station's substructures, but then he just disappeared. I have people combing the area, but we haven't found anything yet. When we do, I'll get word to you. Your… people promised to keep my line of communication to you open."

"I don't feel like they're really my people," Scout said.

"I guess you'd consider them your government," Sergeant Murray said with a hint of distaste. Scout guessed the sergeant considered the government down on the planet a form of mutiny.

"Not really," Scout said. "I was trying to leave this place when we were detained. Isn't there some way to renounce my citizenship or something?"

"If there is, you'd have to pursue that angle from within the Enclave," Sergeant Murray said. Then her desk beeped, a red light flashing in one corner. She dismissed the alert with a wave of her hand, then got to her feet. "We have to get going."

"My stuff," Scout said, realizing she had left her tote in the waiting room.

"We'll send it on to you," Sergeant Murray said.

"My dogs," Scout said pleadingly.

"We will send them on," Sergeant Murray said, and Scout heard regret in her voice but was too angry to care.

"I won't go!" Scout said, looking up at the still-impassive Geeta. "Not without my dogs. I want them, now."

"The Enclave demanded your immediate surrender to their custody; we cannot delay," Sergeant Murray said. "Will you cooperate? Please don't make Ensign Malini use her stunner on you."

"No," Scout said, clutching the chair beneath her tightly. "You can't make me go. I don't even know those people. I want my dogs."

"Your dogs will be safe with us until we can negotiate handing them over," Sergeant Murray said. "Scout, I don't like this. It's being handled in far too rushed a manner. Something is going on. But it's not my place to buck authority. I have to deliver you to Captain Brenner. But I will be in contact, I will be continuing the search for your friend, and I will guard your dogs with my own life if it comes to that."

Scout blinked back hot tears. She looked up again at Geeta. She was still standing there statue-like, but at a nod from the sergeant she pulled a pair of restraints from her belt and bent to fasten them around Scout's wrists. Scout jerked her hands away to hide them behind her back.

"If you don't cooperate, we'll have to deliver you stunned," Sergeant Murray said. "We must get moving."

"Scout," Geeta said. Her voice had an air of command to it, but her eyes, when she bent forward to reach for Scout's wrists a second time, were pleading with her to understand.

Was she the friend Scout was supposed to remember? She and her sister? But what could a pair of ensigns do that the sergeant couldn't? They were barely older than Scout, who was quite powerless in the battle against bureaucracy.

Geeta bit her lip, her eyes widening further.

Scout put out her wrists.

"The dogs are still recovering from the effects of the tranquilizers," Geeta whispered as she fastened the restraints, although the room was so tiny the sergeant must have heard her. "It's not safe to move them right now. But I promise—"

"No more promises," Scout said, then got to her feet. She would go along with what they wanted her to do for now, but once in the Enclave, all bets were off. If the people in the Enclave thought they represented her, then they were going to listen to her demands.

And if not, she had at least one new nugget of information: under the towers were sublevels, and people could move around in the sublevels without being seen. She would find a way to get Liam and her dogs back. Then they would leave this place behind and never return.

Scout wasn't going to be anybody's pawn.

9

GEETA KEPT a hold on Scout's arm, but more to support her if she tripped while her hands were tied than to restrain her. She led her out a door on the far side of the tiny office into a larger room filled with activity, all people in navy-blue jumpsuits like Geeta's or uniforms like the sergeant's, talking in clusters or working at desks. Sergeant Murray emerged from her office behind Geeta and Scout, calling out a few names. By the time Geeta had steered Scout across the room to a wide set of stairs, they had a dozen security workers in navy blue forming a phalanx around them.

The stairs ended in the space between the gateways Scout had passed through briefly before. She even caught one last glimpse of Liam's ship beyond one of the gateways, but Geeta was guiding her in the opposite direction to a bank of elevators. There were five elevators on each side of the little atrium, but Geeta marched up to the larger eleventh door that dominated the far wall. The door opened instantly at her touch and Geeta, Scout, Sergeant Murray, and their dozen guards all poured inside with room to spare.

"Is it far?" Scout asked.

"You know the building your friend was taken to? It's just on the other side of that," Geeta explained. "But there is only one connecting walkway, so we have to circle around to the far side."

The elevator started to move. It felt to Scout like the floor was dropping out from under her and she felt a moment's panic. Geeta was still gripping her arm but changed position to put an arm around her shoulders.

"It's a little disorienting at first," Geeta said. "Because of the spin of the station, you'll be heavier in the lower levels than you are at the tops of the towers. Some people are bothered by that, but others scarcely notice it."

The elevator jolted to a stop, and the doors slid open to reveal a crowded platform next to a train that was just getting moving. Swarms of people in navy-blue or gray jumpsuits with just a few purples and greens dotted among them stood between them and the train.

"We'll have to catch the next one," Geeta said, but Sergeant Murray pulled out a little device and pressed a button. It emitted a long, sustained shriek that got everyone's attention. Even, apparently, the train itself. Not only did the train grind to a halt, but everyone gathered on the platform moved away to give them a clear path to the train doors.

"We're in a hurry," Sergeant Murray said to the dark-skinned man in a gray jumpsuit waiting for them at the train doors. "I'll deal with any forms you need me to submit later. For now, we have to get to the Enclave."

The man—who had looked ready to argue before the sergeant had spoken—just gave a nod and signaled for the doors to close after the sergeant and her entourage brushed past him and boarded the train car.

"Express," Sergeant Murray said to him.

"I know my job," the man said. "We're three minutes out."

Sergeant Murray looked at the time displayed over the train doors. She sighed.

"Express?" Scout whispered to Geeta.

"We'll be blowing past all the stops," Geeta told her. "It's going to wreck the transport schedules and piss a lot of people off, but we have to get you there on time. The Enclave does this all the time. Demands things to happen on an all-but-impossible schedule, so we have to scramble. They keep hoping we'll fail."

"Why do you do it?" Scout asked.

"We need goods from the surface," Geeta said. She seemed like she wanted to say more, but Sergeant Murray shot her a sharp look and she fell silent.

Scout thought of the data disks she had left behind in the tote with her other belongings. She wondered if anyone in security would get curious and try to see what was on them. They were encrypted, but the rebels had been able to unlock them in a few hours. Liam's computer had done it instantaneously, but Scout didn't think the Space Farers had that kind of galactic tech.

Unless, of course, they brought the disks back to Liam's ship and used his computer.

One disk contained the schematics of a massive gun the Planet Dwellers were building, one built specifically to be powerful enough to take out the space station they were all standing in. It had been approaching completion when Scout had left the rebel hideout. She didn't know if the Space Farers even knew of its existence.

The other disk had been about what the Space Farers were up to: deliberately dismantling the satellites designed to protect the surface from coronal mass ejection events. They had also been inflating their population numbers on the census they sent to the surface, the numbers used to determine their allotment of food.

The information would be on the open market soon, the rebels looking to pit one side against the other. Scout didn't know what they hoped to gain by that. But then she never understood why the people on the surface and the people up in orbit had started fighting in the first place. She only knew that if things kept on like they were going, with the Space Farers putting the Planet Dwellers in constant danger by removing the satellites and the Planet Dwellers putting their finishing touches on a space station–annihilating gun, a lot of people were going to die. And the people in a position to stop it didn't seem to care.

She did wonder about that census data, though. The security building had been largely empty where she had been, but Seeta had blamed that on the barricade. If she had been in a part of the building set aside for extra screening for passengers coming from other parts of the galaxy, that made sense.

But there still had been so many people getting on and off ships, and although they had the train car to themselves, the platform had been crowded, and she suspected the car had been emptied for their use just as the people had stepped aside to clear a path for them. From what she could see, this space station was as crowded as any of the cities down on the surface.

Were they claiming even more people than an already large population? Or were there a lot of sparsely populated space stations also in orbit of Amatheon?

Scout lifted her restrained hands to rub at her forehead. The one thought she kept circling back to was her great desire to just be gone. To leave this all behind—the planet, the orbiting space stations, all of it. She hoped that was still possible. She wanted more out of her life than being a pawn. She wanted to do something that mattered.

The train slowed to a halt and Geeta took Scout's arm once more to guide her across another crowded platform to another elevator. This was smaller than the other had been, but Sergeant Murray still packed all fifteen of them into one car before closing the doors. Bodies were pressed up against Scout on all sides. If she fainted, she'd still be on her feet, unable to fall over or collapse.

The elevator rocketed them up at terrific speed. Scout apparently wasn't one of the types who was sensitive to the change in weight, she realized belatedly. Being down at train level hadn't felt any different from being at landing platform level. She closed her eyes, playing back the sensations, but she had been too distracted by all the people around her to notice whether she felt any heavier.

That was probably good, though, in case she had to go down to the sublevels and find Liam herself. The deeper she went, the heavier she'd be. Better if she didn't really notice it.

She was curious how far down she could go. Were there windows on the bottom of the station to look at the galaxy rotating by? Would it be disorienting to see Amatheon tumbling around her?

The elevator lurched to a halt, and one of the guards opened the doors. They all spilled out into another hallway, and Scout gratefully took a deep breath of air. Sergeant Murray was already leading the way at a brisk walk across the hallway to a wide staircase.

There were no people around. At the top of the stairs, little booths were built into the walls on either side, with windows that leaned out into the hall. The guard standing inside the booths could see back down the stairs or up the next, shorter flight of stairs just by leaning forward while remaining behind a protective layer of glass.

And each guard was standing in their little booth with a rifle in their hands.

"Why the guns?" Scout asked. "Why don't the guards with us have guns?"

"They work security; they carry stunners like I do," Geeta said. "You can't see, and it's probably better if you don't try to look, but the platform we're about to step out onto is covered by dozens of watch posts. If anyone from the Enclave makes a single false move, our snipers will fire."

"What good would that do? If your political balance is so precarious, why risk it?"

"We have to," Geeta said. "They have snipers, too."

The shorter flight of stairs led up to a wide balcony. A gentle wind caught Scout's hair as she jogged up the last few steps. The air still had that electric smell to it. Like before a storm, it smelled like the world was waiting for something explosive to happen.

Once they were out of the hallway and out in the open, Scout tipped her head back to stare straight up at the far side of the station again. The rush of vertigo was addicting.

Then she looked at the towers around her. They were shorter than the tower she was in, all except the one directly in front of them. It was a twin to their tower, matching its height, the width of its balcony, everything. Between the two towers was a walkway wide enough for a pair of rovers to drive past each other.

And on the far end of the walkway, Captain Brenner stood amid his own phalanx of guards, watching her approach with a predatory smile.

10

GEETA GUIDED Scout to the middle of the point where balcony became walkway and then stopped. Sergeant Murray was speaking in low tones to the other guards, and they were nodding and moving around the balcony. A few looked up at the tower behind them. Scout followed their gaze but couldn't see exactly what they were looking at. Geeta's hand on her upper arm gave her a reassuring squeeze, reminding her that she was as safe as the security team could make her, but Scout remembered her words, that it would be better not to try to find all the guns aimed at them, and turned back around.

Captain Brenner was waiting for them to get into position with patience so exaggerated Scout could feel disdain coming off him in waves. Scout wondered if he had been born in space or down on the planet. How long had there even been an Enclave? Since the war began, or even before that? For that matter, had the outbreak of war been the start of what the Space Farers called the mutiny, or just the most egregious offense?

"All right," Sergeant Murray said, finally stepping up to Scout's side. "Let's go. Slowly."

"Yes, ma'am," Geeta said. Captain Brenner matched them, step by deliberate step. A woman walked beside him, the Enclave's version of

Geeta, Scout supposed, only this woman was older and probably held a higher rank, just as captain outranked sergeant. Was the mismatch in ranks part of the political dance? A bit of informal communication about priorities? She was more valuable to the Enclave than to the Space Farers? Someone must have decided this was Sergeant Murray's job and not Captain Suze's.

The wind picked up as they neared the center of the walkway, spinning Scout's honey-blonde curls into her eyes. She tried to tuck it back behind her ears, but with her hands tied together, it was awkward.

From the center of the platform, she couldn't see just how high up they were beyond being atop the tallest tower in the area. She thought of how fast the elevator had ascended and how long it had taken to get to the top and decided she was happier not knowing. She had stood at the edge of cliffs in the canyons back home, but they had been nowhere near this tall.

Sergeant Murray stopped walking when they were still about three meters away from Captain Brenner. He too stopped and crossed his arms, still broadcasting that he was waiting. The woman at his side had her hand on something attached to her belt, but made no other move.

"Scout," Sergeant Murray said, so suddenly Scout almost jumped. "This is Captain Mark Brenner of the Enclave. Your well-being is in his hands the moment you step away from me. Captain Brenner, this is Scout Shannon."

"Pleased to meet you, Scout," Captain Brenner said, trying for friendly but missing by quite a bit. "You don't want to know all we've been through to secure your release, but you're here now."

"This is the opposite of a release," Scout said. "I want to stay here, on this side of things."

Captain Brenner scowled briefly, then tried for friendly again. "I'm sure you're feeling more than a little confused by all this. You aren't deliberately attempting treason, are you?"

"Treason?" Scout repeated.

"Defecting to the Space Farers is treason under our government's laws," Captain Brenner said. "I can explain it to you in great depth once we're inside. Come along, girl."

Scout remained where she was. "How soon will you fetch my dogs?"

"Dogs?" Captain Brenner looked to the woman at his side.

"She had two dogs with her," the woman answered, never moving her hand from whatever was on her belt. "We believe they came from the surface."

"Shadow was licensed before the destruction of Sunshine Valley," Scout said. "Gert is a free agent, but they are from the surface, yes."

"You're from Sunshine Valley?" Captain Brenner asked.

"Yes," Scout said.

"And you're talking about defecting? To the people who murdered your family?"

"I want to stay with my dogs until my friend is found and we can all continue on as before," Scout said. "I don't want to have anything to do with Planet Dwellers or Space Farers or rebels either. I don't know how I got caught up in this big political power play."

"No, I don't suppose you do," Captain Brenner said, not bothering to hide his disdain now. "Your arrival has complicated a lot of things, and I cannot allow you to destroy months of negotiations on a whim."

"It's not a whim—"

"No!" Captain Brenner shouted, loud enough to make Scout flinch. It might have been her imagination, but she had the distinct sense of a lot of hands around her moving their guns to a more ready position, fingers on triggers.

"Let's—" Sergeant Murray started to say in a calming voice, but a sudden blare of alarms drowned her out. The woman next to Captain Brenner, who still hadn't moved her hand, was tipping her head, looking for all the world like Shadow listening to something.

"Perimeter breach," she said to the captain.

"Not us," Sergeant Murray said quickly. Captain Brenner scowled.

"It's on our side of the walkway, but it's in a maintenance tunnel with outside access," the woman went on.

"It's not us," Sergeant Murray said again. "You know as well as we do that if we were going to make a move, we'd do it with spacecraft."

Captain Brenner looked up into the center of the space station.

There were ships scattered here and there throughout the open space, but nothing close. Nothing heading their way.

"Obviously it's not us," he said. "Can it be a false alarm?"

"Someone is on the way to check it out now," the woman said.

"Rebels?" Scout said, realizing too late she had said it out loud.

The sergeant and captain both looked her way quizzically. Were there any rebels in space? Or maybe a different group, rebelling *mainly* against the Space Farers as the ones on the surface were rebelling *mainly* against the Planet Dweller government?

"Step across, girl," Captain Brenner said, holding out a hand. "We'll all feel better when we're no longer out in the open."

"Another perimeter breach," the woman said. "What's going on down there?"

"Come on, now!" the captain said to Scout.

She stared at his outstretched hand, but made no move.

Captain Brenner took a step closer to Scout and suddenly the tiles of the walkway floor were a dazzling array of red lights dancing around him.

Laser sights.

"Hold your fire!" he and the sergeant yelled at once. The number of lights doubled, dancing between the two of them. Scout flinched away, pressing up against Geeta.

"It's okay," Geeta said close to her ear.

Then everyone started firing at once. Scout saw the laser sights wink out, leaving behind shattered tile and little clouds of debris. It would almost be hypnotic if it weren't so frightening.

"To the edge!" Geeta shouted, pulling Scout away from the middle of the walkway. The edge of the walkway was a low wall, not much cover, but better than nothing. Scout ran as quickly as she could while bent over with her hands tied, which wasn't as quickly as she would've liked. She was vaguely aware that she was yelling, but the world around her was such a cacophony of sounds she knew it only by the growing rawness of her throat.

Then the toes of her slippered right foot slammed hard into a fractured tile and she was stumbling, running faster in an attempt to catch herself before she fell. She saw Geeta already huddled against the low wall, hands reaching out to catch Scout and pull her to safety.

But when those hands closed on her upper arms, Geeta pivoted, shifting a hand to the waistband of Scout's pants and lifting her off the ground, letting her own momentum take her over the top of the wall. Hands still tied, Scout had no way to catch hold of anything. She kicked out hard and felt one foot impact with Geeta's stomach, but it wasn't enough to stop her body's trajectory.

The bullet-shattered wall passed beneath her and a sudden gust of wind blasted the hair back from her face, leaving her an unobstructed view of the canyon-like expanse between the two towers that went on and on beyond what her eyes could bring into focus.

She had done a lot of looking up since she'd arrived at the station, but this was her first glance down at the streets: tiny vehicles moving in fits and starts, people smaller than ants milling about under the streetlights. It didn't seem real. It was just too miniature and perfect.

Then she started to fall.

11

EVERY THOUGHT in Scout's head just stopped. No words, no images, no feelings could form an adequate response to what was happening to her. She couldn't draw a breath either, but it was the feeling of the gears of her mind suddenly jammed and locked that would have been the most frightening if she could have summoned up the mental power to feel fear.

Would she spend the next several seconds in this blank state until her body reached the bottom?

Then, for the second time that day, she had the sensation of being in an invisible giant's hand. Only the giant wasn't so gentle this time. It wasn't lifting her, safe inside a ship, gently up from the ground, but snatching her out of midair.

At least her mind had unsnapped, and she could resume screaming in terror.

But she couldn't do that forever. She forced herself to stop screaming and just take deep breaths. She wasn't falling, but she wasn't able to sit up either. She was mostly lying on her back, but she wasn't sure what she was feeling beneath her.

She opened her eyes and looked up. The edge of the walkway was a few meters above her head. She rolled onto her side. Tucked underneath the walkway as she was, everything was dark, and she couldn't see what was supporting her. She rolled onto her belly and tried to get a knee underneath her, but the substance below her kept giving way.

A net, Scout suddenly realized, feeling the individual threads of it digging into her body in crisscrosses. A safety net.

Maybe not so safe, Scout decided. The gun battle raged on overhead and bits of walkway were raining down on her, one sharp fragment striking her frighteningly close to her eye. She wasn't out of this yet.

Now that she knew it was a net beneath her, she knew what to do. She couldn't put her arms to her sides, but she could tuck them close to her chest. Then she extended her legs and rolled toward the center of the walkway, the lowest point of the net and the farthest from the gunfight.

She was still in the fix of being unable to crawl over the bouncing net, particularly with her hands still bound together, but at least she could struggle with that task without the fear of shrapnel blinding her.

"Good job, Scout," a voice said out of the darkness. Scout tipped her head back until she saw a flash of candy-red hair.

"Ensign Tonnelier?" she said.

"Call me Emilie," the ensign answered. "But first hold out your hands."

"Geeta Malini threw me over the side," Scout said as Emilie took a pair of cutters from her utility belt and snipped away the restraints. They fell through the holes in the net, dancing away on the whims of the wind. Better them than her.

Her stomach clenched at the sight of the drop below her. Would she have reached the bottom yet if she had missed the net?

"Why did she try to kill me?" Scout asked, then looked up sharply at Emilie. That look that had passed between the two ensigns—what had it meant?

"All part of the plan," Emilie said with a lopsided grin as she stowed the cutters. "Follow me."

Scout didn't know why anyone would spend a lot of time crawling around in nets, but Emilie looked like she had, scampering delicately over the surface at high speed. Scout had seen less graceful spiders navigating their own webs. Scout followed the same path with more difficulty, not even sure where they were heading. Back to the tower she had come from. That was all she could tell. Not to the Enclave. That was something.

Then she got closer and saw the open hatch tucked just under the walkway above, all but invisible in the darkness. Emilie was already inside, waiting for Scout to draw closer before extending a hand.

"Something set off a perimeter breach alarm," Scout said as Emilie pulled her inside the tiny space and closed the hatch behind her. A panel behind Emilie was giving off some dim light from a few of its indicators, but not enough for Scout to see more than the outline of Emilie's crouching body.

"That was me," Emilie said. "Some parts of this plan were more improv than others."

"You wanted all this shooting?"

"Not specifically. We did need a diversion."

"We?" Scout asked.

"Come on," Emilie said, ignoring the question. "I need a better vantage." Scout saw the silhouette of her hand going up to adjust the temple of her glasses, then two little lights flared to life just over Emilie's ears. Scout was momentarily blinded until Emilie turned her head.

What Scout had taken as a tiny space, perhaps for storage, turned out to be a square shaft, although Scout could only see bits of it as Emilie started crawling down it. The light from her glasses must have been meant to illuminate close-up work in dark spaces, not to light anyone's way, so Scout couldn't see more than a few hand spans in front of Emilie, and most of that was quickly blocked by Emilie's body. But Emilie seemed to know just where she was going, crawling through the low shaft as nimbly as she had scampered over the net. Scout struggled to keep up.

The shaft crossed another, similar shaft and then ended at the bottom of a ladder. Emilie climbed up, quickly disappearing from sight and taking the only source of light with her.

Scout felt for the rungs of the ladder and started climbing. The horizontal shafts had been large enough to sit up in, if not walk, but this vertical shaft was round and barely large enough for Scout to climb through, and Scout wasn't all that big. What were these shafts used for? Her back scraped repeatedly against the wall of the shaft behind her. She wished she had light-up glasses.

Her hand reached for the next rung and grasped a few times at emptiness before there was once more a blinding light in her eyes. A hand closed around hers, helping her up onto the floor.

"Too bright," Scout said, flinching against the light.

"Sorry," Emilie said, and the lights on her glasses winked out. But there was another source of light dimly filtering in through a grate a short distance away. Emilie and Scout crawled towards it. Scout could hear voices shouting, one of them Sergeant Murray's, and realized they were overlooking the long balcony. The gunfire had stopped. She pressed her face close to the vent and saw the walkway off to her right. Sergeant Murray and Captain Brenner were still standing in the middle of the space, arguing with each other.

"Geeta," Emilie said, and Scout searched until she saw Ensign Malini standing with a group of navy-blue guards. "They aren't detaining her. Good. If anyone had seen her throw you over, she'd be done for."

"Did anyone get shot?" Scout asked. She didn't see any bodies on the ground or anyone bleeding.

"I don't think so," Emilie said. "Good. Good." She sounded like she was checking things off of a mental list.

"It's good that no one got hurt," Scout allowed. "But what's with throwing me over the side? Without warning me?"

"Obviously, we couldn't warn you. We're being watched all the time."

"Like now?" Scout shot back.

"Geeta is being watched. I know how to dodge surveillance," Emilie said. Then that lopsided grin was back. "We all have skills."

"Who's we?" Scout asked.

"The three of us: me, Geeta, and Seeta," Emilie said. "Seeta has an in with the assistant to one of the uppity-ups. I guess you could say her skill is connections. He passed along the word of how the negotiations were going to Seeta. As you know, not good. Too fast, wrong conclusion. So the three of us decided to step in."

"I don't understand," Scout said, rubbing her head.

"We couldn't let you get sucked into the Enclave. Not with what you know. And with who you know."

"But I don't know anyone here," Scout said. "Just you people. And Liam."

"I mean down on the surface."

Scout frowned. "Again—"

"The rebels. You know the rebels," Emilie said, her grin edging ever wider. Perhaps a hair too wide; her glee was starting to freak Scout out a little bit.

"What do you want with the rebels?" Scout asked. She hoped Emilie and her friends weren't as naively deluded as she had been up until a week ago. Before she had met the galactic marshal Gertrude Bauer, she had spent all of her time waiting for the rebellion to discover her, to take her in and let her earn her place among them. Gertrude had changed her mind about that. Her future was in Galactic Central, doing something so much more amazing than agitating unrest and robbing trains.

After Gertrude had died, while Scout was waiting for Liam—who had half a galaxy to cross to get to her—she had finally met the rebels she had been idolizing from afar.

To say they had proved a disappointment would be an understatement. Aside from how she herself had been treated, the man in charge of the group she had fallen in with had been dangerously deranged.

Still, he had had a boss whom Scout had never met. There might be more going on than she knew.

But what did Emilie know?

"There's no time to go into all of this now. Plus, Seeta is better at explaining this stuff than I am. She'll tell you everything."

"Where is she?" Scout asked, looking around. They weren't in another long shaft, just a tiny space behind the vent.

"Not here, obviously," Emilie said. "She's back at the apartment. We have to get to her."

"Okay," Scout said tiredly.

"No good," Emilie said, shaking her head.

"What's no good?"

"Your attitude," Emilie said. "I know you're tired and stressed, but I need you to get charged up. I'm going to need absolutely everything you can give me, every bit of your attention and judgment and quickness."

"For what?" Scout asked.

Emilie leaned forward as if she wanted to be sure Scout didn't miss the wideness of her grin. "Scout Shannon, you and I are going to cross the most densely populated, heavily surveilled space you've ever ventured into. And not one person is going to notice us. We're going to be invisible."

12

SCOUT FOLLOWED Emilie back down the ladder and through a maze of shafts. She lost her sense of direction after the third or fourth turn and gave up trying to keep a mental map. She just focused on the soles of Emilie's shoes in front of her. They were white rubber with red hearts at the balls of her feet. The canvas tops were white and black stripes and extended past her ankles. They even had little zippered pockets on the side. Scout found that sort of feature very useful. She liked having lots of pockets.

The air was cold and thick with the dust stirred up by Emilie's hands and knees, and Scout sneezed several times in rapid succession, so hard she had to stop crawling until she was done.

Emilie was looking back over her shoulder at her. "Get that out of your system now," she said.

"It's not like I can control it," Scout said, sniffling.

"Actually you can," Emilie said, but rather than explaining the trick to that, she continued on.

But she was moving a bit slower now, stirring up less dust. Scout sniffled again from time to time but didn't have another sneezing fit.

Emilie turned down a cross shaft that ended in a little door. There was a number pad in the wall next to the door and Emilie entered a long series of numbers, pausing before continuing more than once. Then she sat down to wait.

"What's this?" Scout asked.

"Elevator to the ground floor," Emilie said.

"That's an elevator? It's so tiny."

"It's meant for gear, but we'll fit," Emilie said. Scout could hear something arriving on the other side of the door. Emilie turned a crank to open the door, which slid up by jerky degrees as she cranked. When it reached the top, Emilie crawled inside the very tiny box, then turned to hold a hand out for Scout to join her.

"I don't think we're both going to fit," Scout said.

"You might have to sit on my lap a little," Emilie allowed. She made grasping motions with her extended hand.

Scout ducked inside, tucking her feet close to her and, indeed, half sitting on Emilie's lap. Emilie had to wrap an arm around her and pull her closer to get all of her body inside the box. Then she had to crank the door shut again from this side. The motion of Emilie's arm was pushing Scout's head up against the roof of the box, bending her neck uncomfortably. At last, the door was shut and Emilie's hands locked around Scout.

"Stay tucked in tight," Emilie warned. "There's no door on this side."

"So what's that mean?" Scout asked, trying to see the doorway behind her.

"The wall is going to be rushing past on that side. You can't fall out of the box, but hitting that moving wall can't be good. Not at the speed we'll be going."

Before Scout could ask how fast that was, she felt Emilie let go with one of her hands to thrust quickly at a button. Then they were plummeting, like the elevator mechanism had just let them go. This couldn't be normal. And they kept speeding up. How long was it possible to keep accelerating? They'd be in free fall soon.

Emilie was screaming and laughing, clearly having the ride of her life. Her arms were hugging Scout tight, keeping her clear of the open side. But that wasn't the only potential for injury, Scout soon discovered. She kept her hands pressed up against the roof of the box, trying to keep her neck from snapping.

Then the box started decelerating, braking hard and driving Scout down onto Emilie with enough force to knock the wind out of her. Scout supposed she should feel bad, but really, she was just grateful to no longer have Emilie shrieking her delight so close to her ear.

"Okay, quiet now," Emilie said as the box slowed to a halt. As if Scout had been making a sound. Emilie cranked the door open but quickly grasped Scout again to keep her from spilling out of the tight space.

"Let me go," Scout whispered.

"Make sure it's clear first," Emilie said. "I can see a little from here, but I can't poke my head out."

"Aren't we just in another maintenance shaft?" Scout asked, but then she felt a cool breeze blowing past her arm nearest the opening. "We're outside?"

"Back alley," Emilie said. "But still, make sure it's clear."

Scout tensed up her arms and legs, getting a sense of where she was in the space. Then she turned at the waist, bracing her hands on the roof of the box nearer the opening, and leaned forward. It was awkward, and only Emilie, still holding her tightly, kept her from spilling headfirst onto the pavement, but she managed to poke just the top of her head out of the elevator and look around.

They were in a dark alley. She could see lights on the streets in both directions, but nothing where they were. The elevator had stopped half a meter off the ground, pavement stained in places as if haunted by the ghosts of spills past. A few scraps of debris were blowing around in the soft breeze, food wrappers and… were those the restraints Emilie had cut off of her?

"Anything?" Emilie asked.

Scout gave the scene one last survey. "There are two trucks parked nearby. The engines are running, but I don't see anybody around."

"Good enough," Emilie said and held onto Scout until she had a foot out of the elevator and on the ground. Emilie unfolded herself after.

"Now what?" Scout asked, looking toward one lighted street and then the other. They looked the same to her: both busy roads filled with motorized traffic and plenty of pedestrians. At least no one was looking their way.

"Here," Emilie said, reaching up to put a headband on Scout's head.

"What is it?" Scout asked as Emilie adjusted something on the front of the band.

"Fashion accessory," Emilie said. "Also scrambles your image on surveillance. I have the same in my glasses. It looks like a glitch or something flaring a reflection of light. It's not perfect; anyone really looking for us will obviously track down two people they can't quite see who keep appearing together on cameras, but it will let us skate past the casual detection."

"But people looking at us can see us," Scout said. "Do I look foreign?"

Emilie looked her over. "Nah. But if they put out an alert, it will include an image of you wearing all that. We'll change it up first opportunity. In the meantime, I'm curious why traffic over here stopped moving. I'm going to take a peek." She walked close to the wall until she got to the end of the alley. She leaned one shoulder against the building and looked straight into the rush of people walking on the pavement. She wasn't trying to hide, more trying to appear like someone looking for a friend they'd lost in the crowd. Scout crept up behind her to look over her shoulder.

"Guards in the street," Scout said. A dozen or so were holding back traffic, a few more walking back and forth across the road, searching the ground for something.

Scout looked up and saw a single walkway far above. She let her eyes sweep down the tower across the street, all the way to street level. There didn't appear to be any doors or windows the entire length.

"I think they're looking for you," Emilie said, catching Scout's arm and drawing her back into the darkness of the alley.

"They're going to know something's up. Is Geeta in danger?" Scout asked.

"Geeta can handle herself," Emilie said as she looked all around the alley.

"Do we take the other street, then?" Scout asked, but even as she did, she saw a pair of guards moving through the crowds there. Like Captain Brenner's assistant, they kept one hand on something on their belts as they pushed past the other people on the pavement.

"No, I have a better idea," Emilie said and pointed to one of the idling trucks. There was a pile of fruits and vegetables painted on the side. "I bet this goes to the marketplace."

"We can't hide in it," Scout said, looking inside the open back of the truck. "They'll see us when they're putting stuff in here."

"Quick, under it," Emilie said, catching Scout's arm, and they dropped down to the filthy pavement and rolled under the truck. A pair of boots walked up to the back of the truck and their owner put something heavy inside with a loud grunt, then walked around to the front of the truck and swung open the driver's side door. The door shut with a slam. "Now!" Emilie hissed, and Scout scrambled after her to climb into the back of the truck. She barely got her second foot off the ground before the truck started backing up. Emilie pulled her further inside, holding on to keep her from falling back out as the truck braked hard, then accelerated.

Then they were out of the dark alley. The bright streetlights bathed over them and Scout crouched behind a crate that was strapped to the side of the truck to keep it from shifting as the truck moved. Good thing, too; the driver did everything in hurried jerks: starting, stopping, darting from one lane to the next and then back again.

Emilie was grinning again, keeping her balance with mere fingertips touching the crate beside her. Scout on the opposite side of the truck was holding on with both hands to heavy-duty straps hanging from the sides of the crates.

The truck took a turn and Scout got a momentary glimpse of the guards scattered under the walkway. They were now waving traffic through, having abandoned the search.

"They're going to figure out what happened," Scout said.

"They probably got as far as the net and the shafts already," Emilie said, still grinning. "Don't worry about it. They will search the building first. Even with drones, that's going to take some time. Only when they still haven't found you will they disseminate your image with a 'be on the lookout,' and by then I'll have changed you up a bit."

Scout had a sudden image of herself with candy-colored hair. Surely there wasn't time for that.

The truck continued on down the busy road. Scout longed to see more of the world around her but was too aware of the vehicles traveling close to them. Would a girl in the back of a vegetable truck be an odd sight? Emilie seemed certain her image wasn't out there yet, but she didn't want to make any kind of impression on anyone's mind that they might remember again later.

It was maddening. Slouched low between the crates, she only got glimpses of the buildings. Occasionally she saw people moving past the windows, but mostly her only impressions were just of featureless towers thrusting up into the sky. Much the same as she'd seen before, only then she'd been looking down and now she was looking up.

Emilie was staring straight ahead, occasionally tapping her temple as if in thought. But as much as she was facing Scout, her eyes weren't focused on her, and Scout realized what she was actually tapping was the stem of her glasses.

Her glasses must be like the mirror lenses the galactic marshal Gertrude Bauer had worn. They allowed her to read like a tablet what appeared to everyone else to be a featureless slab of plastic for starters. They had also told her information about the world she was looking at: temperature and distance and light intensity and things like that.

"What are you looking at?" Scout asked her.

"News feeds," Emilie said. "I'm setting some alerts. I want to know when they go wide with the search."

"Good idea," Scout said. "Were you right? Are we going to the marketplace?"

"Yes, we're nearly there," Emilie said.

"What is the driver going to think when he sees us running out of the back of his truck?" Scout asked, again worried about someone remembering her later.

"If we're quick and crafty, he won't see us," Emilie said. "The trick is to jump out before he gets to where he's going."

"We're going to jump out of a moving truck?" Scout asked, incredulous.

Emilie grinned again, particularly maniacally this time. "I mean, we'll let it slow down a bit around a corner or something."

Scout gulped, but said nothing. She was getting the impression that even if there were an easier way to get around, Emilie might not take it. She was just having far too much fun doing it this way.

On the other hand, Scout could think of no one better to help her find Liam so she could get her dogs and get off this eternally dark space station. If anyone knew all the hidey-holes that lurked in the subbasements, it would be a girl like Emilie.

13

EMILIE MUST HAVE SEEN familiar landmarks because she stopped tapping at the temple of her glasses and sat forward, squatting on her toes with splayed fingers on the floor of the truck for balance.

If the driver braked hard, Scout would be on her own.

But Emilie kept her balance better than Scout thought possible, even when the truck took a turn to start down a curving ramp. Emilie edged closer to the open hatch of the truck. Now that they had left the main road, there were no vehicles behind them. Scout was getting an "it's now or never" vibe and put her feet under her so that, like Emilie, she was squatting and not sitting.

"Get ready," Emilie said to Scout. Scout kept hold of the strap on the crate closest to the back of the truck with both hands, but moved her feet and body closer to the edge. Emilie was leaning forward, her head over the pavement passing in a blur beneath them.

Then the truck slowed to make a tighter turn.

"Now!" Emilie said, springing out of the truck. Scout was slower, having to mentally force her hands to unclench around the crate strap. The truck was halfway through the turn when the driver hit the accelerator again and Scout went tumbling out the back end.

Emilie rushed forward to not so much catch Scout as put her own body in the way to break her fall. They both went down in a tangle of arms and legs, Emilie once more laughing in sheer joy.

There was a shriek that echoed against the canyon-like walls of the ramp: a vehicle grinding to a halt to avoid running them over. The driver leaned out his window to swear at them, and only grew more irate at Emilie's laughter. Scout clung close to Emilie, keeping her head ducked so the driver couldn't see her face. He sped off the moment they had stumbled out of his way. Clearly, people weren't supposed to be walking in this place, even though there was no place to walk except on the road.

"The train station is on the far side of the marketplace," Emilie said, suddenly serious again. Scout realized most of that laughter had been for that guy's benefit. Two giggling teenage girls didn't draw as much attention as two girls looking shifty, especially if he had been close enough to see them jump out of the back of the truck. "Keep your head down like you've been doing. I'll pick up some things on our way through, but don't worry about where I'm at. Just keep walking and I'll catch up. Okay?"

"You're not going to leave me?" Scout asked.

"Of course not," Emilie said. "We'll draw less attention if we don't seem like we're together."

"But what if I lose you?" Scout asked.

Emilie leaned closer. Scout thought the glasses she wore might be magnifying her eyes a bit. They looked so huge and wide, but there was no doubt about the seriousness in them. "You just keep walking. *I'm* not going to lose *you*," she said.

At the bottom of the ramp, they reached a road with a sidewalk. Just a few steps away was a narrow staircase heading up. Emilie ran up the steps and Scout followed. The walls were close on either side of the stairs, and the steps were so steep Scout had to keep her eyes on her feet. When she reached the top, she found herself in what she took for the marketplace equivalent of a back alley. There was no one around and she could finally get a good look at the world around her without drawing notice.

The marketplace was made up of row after row of semipermanent stalls, built from components that could be locked together or unlocked and stacked flat to be moved. They used the same building materials all over back home. She was looking at the back side of a long row of stalls, but all the doors on this side were closed. She could hear people, swarms of people, but it was quiet where they were, if the ground was a bit sticky.

Emilie led the way between two of the stalls and then out into a sea of people, letting the flow of the crowd guide them along in the open space between the stalls. Everyone was either wearing color-coded jumpsuits or the two-piece uniforms that Scout guessed meant they were higher up the corporate structure. Many had added caps or scarves to give them more of an individual look. A very few had hair like Emilie's that stood out starkly in the crowd.

Emilie left her side almost at once. Scout kept her head down as much as she could but followed the progress of that bright red hair through the crowd out of the corners of her eyes. Emilie paused at a stall and returned almost at once, draping a long silky scarf over Scout's head and around her shoulders. She disappeared again and Scout lifted a corner of the scarf to admire the color. It was all blue, but dozens of shades of blue that faded one into another with no real pattern. It reminded her of the ocean of her home world as she had just seen it from orbit that morning. Immense, but with depths and shallows.

Emilie passed close by again, this time putting another bundle of fabric in Scout's hands. Without slowing her steps, Scout shook it out, saw it was a long skirt with a beaded waistband and hem, and wrapped it around her hips and tied it shut. The clothes she had been wearing on the walkway were now completely covered. The beads on the skirt clinked pleasantly as she walked, although the color—somewhere between burgundy and greenish purple—wasn't really to her taste. She would bet Emilie had chosen it because Scout could put it on without stopping her walk across the marketplace.

The shoes Emilie brought next were trickier to put on between steps, but Scout managed it with a bit of hopping. She was pleased they were shoes like Emilie's, with high tops and ankle pockets, the canvas uppers blue to match her scarf with little white dots.

She wondered if she was going to be able to keep them after they got to where they were going.

Scout frowned when she realized she was coming to the end of the marketplace, but didn't slow her steps. She only had a few more seconds to decide what path to take, but she could see no clue about which way she should go. There was no signage pointing out a train station, nothing.

Then someone brushed past her shoulder. At first, Scout flinched away, fearing the sudden appearance of a restraining hand on her shoulder, but it was only Emilie passing her at a walk so fast it was nearly a jog. She dodged around the corner of the last stall selling something deep fried that smelled spicy and fantastic, and Scout's stomach growled.

When Scout rounded the corner she saw another flight of steps, this one wider and shallower, curving around a fountain and terraced plantings to a wide paved area. People were gathered around tables and chairs, eating together under intensely bright lights. There were stunted trees growing out of open patches in the pavement and a few more sad little flower beds. The lights must have been grow lights, but they didn't seem to be doing the job. Either that or everything trying to grow here needed more water than they were giving it. Nothing was exactly thriving.

Emilie skipped up another wide staircase and disappeared through the open doorway of the tower that overlooked the marketplace. Scout hurried her steps, anxious not to lose sight of Emilie.

Inside the tower was an immense atrium. Here Scout's sense of hurry did fail her. She stopped, head tipping further and further back as she looked up through a shaft that extended up through the heart of the tower all the way to the top. She almost thought she could see past a window crowning the top of the building and beyond into the center of the space station, but perhaps she was only imagining the floating specks of distant craft.

When she at last dropped her gaze, she realized she had lost track of Emilie. Her heart started to pound, but she forced herself to appear outwardly calm, moving to the side so she wasn't blocking anyone's way as she had been while staring up into the building. Then she looked around in little glimpses, trying not to be obvious about it.

No sign of candy-red hair, but she did see a picture of a train with an arrow pointing down an escalator. Scout headed in that direction, holding one edge of the scarf next to her face to keep it from slipping off her head as people brushed past her.

The escalator ended on a train platform with a train already there, but no one was moving. Everyone who had needed to get on or off had already done so. Scout still saw no sign of Emilie. She ran up to the train, looking in the windows compartment after compartment. The train closed its doors and started to move and Scout was fighting back real panic now. Where was she?

She had run out of compartments. Had Emilie not even come down here?

Scout had just turned to head back up the escalator when two strong hands closed down on her shoulders and pulled her clear off the platform.

"Well, *you* almost got left behind!" Emilie said as Scout struggled to get her footing. They were on a tiny metal grate hanging off the back of the train that was moving ever faster beneath them. Scout seized at the railing that would be woefully inadequate at catching her body if she started to fall.

"Can't we ride inside?" Scout asked, clutching the railing as tightly as she could. Emilie just sat down on the grate, fingers threading through the openings but not quite grasping anything.

"Not now," Emilie said, shouting over the rising wind around them. "The alerts just went out. Best not to risk it."

The scarf around Scout's shoulders started to lift up into the air and she had to take a hand off the railing to catch it. As loud as it was on the back of a train hurtling through a tunnel, she thought she could hear Emilie chuckling.

As soon as the train stopped speeding up, it started slowing down.

"Not our stop yet," Emilie told her. The train stopped with a small lurch and Scout could hear the clang of doors opening and the soft roar of people moving on and off. She took advantage of the quiet moment to knot the scarf tightly around her neck, then grasped the railing with both hands as the train began to roll once more.

No one on the platform seemed to notice them. A few were standing around waiting for another train, but they all had their eyes on the tablets in their hands, or were talking together in pairs, or were gathered in a group around a man playing some sort of stringed instrument Scout had never seen before. She liked the jangly sound of it, although she couldn't hear what he was singing as his voice was overlapping itself in echoes.

Then they were back in the dark tunnel, gaining speed.

"Next stop!" Emilie yelled to her over the wind. Scout just nodded. She was more than ready for this part of the journey to end.

The train slowed to a stop. The platform wasn't in view, but there was a narrow walkway that ran alongside the tracks, and Emilie hopped down onto that. Scout stepped down beside her. Emilie waited until the train had pulled away before she climbed up onto the platform, turning to extend a hand to Scout.

The people ahead of them that had gotten out of the compartments of the train were funneling onto the escalator, but Emilie took Scout's hand and guided her down a side hallway. The door at the end of the hallway was stuck fast and Emilie had to slam into it with her shoulder before it banged open to reveal a staircase.

"This is our building," she said to Scout as they jogged side by side up the stairs. "It's probably extra important no one thinks they spotted you here, since we have nowhere else to hide you."

"Okay," Scout said.

"So that's me saying I'm sorry for making you run up twenty-four flights of stairs," Emilie said as they turned at the first landing and headed up the second flight.

"Oh," Scout said, resisting the temptation to look up. Best to stay focused on one step at a time.

"Seeta is making dinner already," Emilie told her. "And she's an excellent cook. In case you, like me, find butter chicken particularly motivating."

"Never had it," Scout said, already losing her breath.

"Well," Emilie said between breaths. "It's worth running up twenty-four flights of stairs for."

Scout mustered up a smile in response. If she had breath left for chatting, she'd be telling Emilie how amazing the shoes were. How had Emilie gotten a pair that fit so perfectly without ever really looking at Scout's feet? Coincidence? Scout has always worn shoes either too large or too small. It was weird not to feel something rubbing, to worry whether a forming blister was going to pop before or after she got to the end of this staircase.

Of course, the twenty-fourth floor was nowhere near the top of the staircase. When they reached the door with that number painted on it, Scout looked up at all the rows after rows of stairs above them, then the fraction of that below them.

"I know," Emilie said, winded but still grinning. "Good thing we aren't rich." She pointed up with a thumb and Scout guessed that meant the higher up the tower you went, the richer the tenants. "Wait here for a sec," Emilie said, then slipped through the numbered door.

Scout unknotted the scarf from around her now-sweaty neck and fluttered it out. She had wrinkled it a bit, but that just made it look more like ripples on water. She liked it almost as much as the shoes.

"Okay, come on," Emilie whispered, beckoning her from the door. Scout tiptoed after her, down a long, dimly lit hallway of closed doors to one that had been left standing half open. Emilie stepped aside to let Scout in first, swiveling her head to look up and down the hall, but no one had seen them.

The smell of chicken and spices washed over her. Then it was Seeta herself flinging her arms around Scout and hugging her tight like a fond friend she had been too long parted from.

"Thank goodness!" Seeta said. "Oh, thank goodness you're safe!"

14

SCOUT LOOKED over Seeta's shoulder at the room around her and hoped that the apartment, like Liam's ship, had extra features hidden behind the walls. Otherwise, she didn't know how anyone could live in a room with a door on one end and a tiny sink built into the wall opposite. It was completely dominated by the table built into the floor. A portable cooker was set up on the end of the table closest to the sink, a large wok-like pan set on the dark red ring, little jets of steam escaping from under the lid. A round, white pot with a locked-down lid was sitting next to it. Plates and forks were stacked in the middle of the table, four of each.

Seeta let Scout go, bustling to the far end of the table to check on the food. Emilie nudged Scout further into the room and then closed the door behind them.

"You both live here?" Scout asked.

"All three," Emilie said.

"But don't worry. We have room for a fourth." Seeta was smiling brightly, but Scout couldn't see how that could possibly be true. Then Seeta turned to look at Emilie and her face went all stern. "Falling off the walkway? How could you let that happen? I saw the video on the news feed and I was horrified."

"*You* were horrified," Scout mumbled to herself.

"It was the only way," Emilie said. "Geeta and I thought it through very carefully."

"It can't have been the only way," Seeta said. "There must have been a thousand better places to extract her between the security building and the walkway."

"No," Emilie said, shaking her head firmly. "Captain Brenner had to see it. If he didn't see it, he wouldn't believe it. He's still going to make trouble, sure, but this way he can't exactly blame our side."

"There had to be another way," Seeta said, but Emilie just shrugged. She turned back to Scout and her face was warmly friendly once more. "Can I get you anything?"

"Do you have jolo?" Scout asked hopefully.

"Not at the moment," Seeta said. "Would tea do?"

"Tea is fine," Scout said.

Seeta turned to the sink and touched the wall above it. As Scout had suspected, a cabinet snapped open, and Seeta took down an electric kettle and filled it with water and set it to boil next to the cooking ring. Emilie reached behind Scout and made a bench appear, and Scout sank down gratefully. Her legs were killing her.

"Geeta is on her way up," Emilie announced as she sat down beside Scout.

"Oh, good," Seeta said, looking immensely relieved. "I was worried about her, too." The kettle beeped just as she was filling a little teapot with loose-leaf tea. She added the boiling water and left it to steep, then turned back to the sink, opening another hidden cabinet to retrieve a mug. She dropped a few cubes of sugar inside, then squatted down to open a small cabinet beside the sink and retrieve a little container that turned out to be milk when she poured it into the mug. She added the tea, stirred the whole thing with a little brown spoon, and pushed it across the table to Scout.

"That's Seeta's special blend," Emilie said, resting her elbow on the table and her head on her hand to watch Scout take her first sip. "The spoon is chocolate. The milk is from the best bio-construct that simulates a cow."

"Emilie," Seeta chided. "Gross."

"I'm just saying," Emilie protested. "There's barely any tea in it. But she calls it tea anyway, and we all pretend like she didn't just make herself a decadent liquid dessert."

Scout took a tentative sip. The melting chocolate from the spoon coated her tongue, then melted away to let her experience the force of really strong black tea. The effect wasn't quite like jolo, but it was still pretty good.

"That's lovely," she said and Seeta beamed.

Then the door opened. Geeta slipped through, quickly shutting the door behind her.

"Someone in the hall?" Emilie asked.

"Just being cautious," Geeta said. She looked wrung out, but she brightened when she saw Scout with her hands curled around one of Seeta's mugs. Then her face fell again into an expression of crushing guilt. "I'm so sorry."

"I gather it was the only way," Scout said as diplomatically as she could, given that she had literally been thrown off a building.

"I wish I could have at least warned you," Geeta said. "Although maybe that would have made it harder for you."

Scout pondered whether that was true. She had to admit, if she had been forewarned, she likely wouldn't have stepped out onto the walkway at all. They would have had to drag her. She supposed she would have aroused suspicions.

The white lidded pot on the table next to the cooker chimed softly and Seeta took off the lid to let a cloud of steam escape.

"I can only stay long enough to eat," Geeta said. "We are on double shifts until Scout is found."

"I'll dish you up first," Seeta said, putting several spoonfuls of rice on one of the plates, then topping it with chunks of chicken from the other pot. The spicy smell made Scout's mouth water, although the reddish-orange color of the sauce clinging to the chicken made her worry it might be a bit too spicy.

"When will they give up hunting for me?" Scout asked.

"When they have proof that you've gone," Geeta said between mouthfuls. "Once we have your friend and get you all back to the ship and off the space station, there's no reason not to be sure they know where you are at that point. Beyond their reach."

"So that's your plan? To get Liam and I back to the ship?" Scout asked.

"Hopefully," Geeta said. "Unfortunately, there's still no sign of him."

"But you are looking?" Scout asked.

"Of course," Geeta said, affronted. "Sergeant Murray told you no lies. She's doing everything she can. Even some things she technically shouldn't."

Seeta set plates full of food in front of Emilie and Scout and then handed them forks. Scout took a tentative bite. Then she saw Emilie watching her and gave her a thumbs-up. She wasn't sure anything was worth running up twenty-four flights of stairs for, but it was still pretty good, the spices lending a complexity of flavors without being burning hot.

"I've got to run," Geeta said, shoveling the last of her food into her mouth. "Just wanted to see you were safe. Seeta will bring you up to speed."

"Wait!" Scout said as Geeta reached for the door handle. "What about my dogs?"

"Last I heard, still sleeping off the effects," Geeta said.

"Some of the components of the tranquilizer had the potential to do long-term neurological damage," Seeta explained. "It's lucky for you they got attention when they did. The techs administered countering agents, but it's better for the dogs to be sleeping until all of that chemical stuff is done happening."

"They'll be fine where they are," Geeta promised her. "The Enclave doesn't care about them, only about you. When we have an out for you, we'll just pick them up and send them along. The dogs are the easy part of all this."

"Thank you," Scout said. She hoped she sounded sincere and not like she was still angry about being thrown off a building.

Geeta nodded, then was gone.

Scout turned back to Seeta and Emilie. "You three risked a lot to keep me out of the Enclave. Why? What do you expect from me?"

"We know what you know," Seeta said. "We suspected our government was lying about our numbers. It's crowded here, but there are other stations no one hears from anymore. I'm betting they're empty. That census data you had with you is proof."

"You read my data disks," Scout guessed. "But I didn't leave them behind until I was on my way to the Enclave, and you were already planning to rescue me then. So when did you read them? While I was in the medical pod?"

"No," Seeta said, glancing up at Emilie.

Emilie took a moment to finish chewing before talking. "No, I got it off the ship," she said. "I have some extra programs on my tablet. When I pull the nav data, which is part of my job, I grab anything else that looks interesting. Which technically isn't."

"Why? Certainly not idle curiosity. Are you guys some kind of spies?" Scout asked.

"We don't work for anybody," Seeta said. "We just feel uneasy about a lot of stuff, and we're trying to figure out what's really going on. Like the census thing."

"We didn't even know about the shield satellites being dismantled," Emilie said. "That's downright evil."

"You have no idea," Scout said. "During the last coronal mass ejection event, I was too far out in the hills to get to a city in time. I had to take shelter in an underground bunker with seven other people. I was the only one to walk out alive. Me and my dogs. Do you know your government sent assassins who look like normal twelve-year-olds to target people in our government?"

"We don't have a government," Seeta said. "We're employees of the Tajaki trade dynasty. We have a management structure, but not a government."

"You down on the planet weren't supposed to have one either," Emilie said. "That was one of the first interesting tidbits we dug up, back when we were all still in school. The Tajaki trade family owns this whole planet since it was discovered. They sent colonists to exploit it, but the colonists had other ideas. They broke a bunch of laws, declaring themselves an independent state when they don't own the land they're standing on just to start."

"I don't understand any of this. What is the Tajaki trade dynasty?"

"We don't know everything ourselves. First off, it's hard to get information about what's going on in the rest of the galaxy," Seeta said. "It's carefully controlled. Our schools teach no history."

"Ours only teach history since landfall," Scout said. "Or at least that was all I ever learned about. I didn't go back to school after the rock dropped from space destroyed my city."

"That was another reason we reached out to you," Seeta said. "We have that in common. We three met when we were in school here on *Amatheon Orbiter 1*, but none of us are from here."

"I came from *Amatheon Orbiter 7*," Emilie said. "Seeta and Geeta were from *Orbiter 9*."

"Both were destroyed by guns firing up from the surface," Seeta said. "We lost our families the same day you lost yours."

"And now they are building a bigger gun," Scout said.

"Yes, we saw that too," Seeta said.

"Are you going to tell your people? Management or whatever?" Scout asked. "Is there anything you can do in self-defense?"

"The best defense is preemptive offense," Emilie said. "That's how they think. We really don't want them to know this."

"Someone has to know," Scout said. "Liam said he knew people in Galactic Central who could help. Who wanted to help if it meant averting a war. But I don't know who they are or how to find them."

"But you know the rebels," Emilie said.

"The rebels," Scout sighed. "I don't know who is actually in charge, but the cell I was with was run by a man who had started going mad. I mean, really crazy. He lost his wife in the war, but that was twelve years ago. There was something more going on with him. I think he was addicted to something, and when he couldn't get it, the withdrawals started making him volatile."

"Maybe you fell in with a bad group?" Emilie said. She sounded like she needed to maintain hope in the rebellion as a force for good.

"I don't know, maybe," Scout said. "But there's no point in trying to contact them with any of this. They already know. They have copies of the data disks, too. They are hoping to sell each side's secrets to the highest bidder. I don't know where that will lead, but I can't imagine it's going to be anywhere good."

"So what do we do?" Emilie asked Seeta. Seeta looked down at her uneaten food glumly.

"Tensions are rising all over," Scout said.

"Yes," Seeta agreed. "Management here is trying to strong-arm your government into disbanding, so we'll all be employees in the same management structure again. But I think that became an impossibility after the war broke out. But they aren't going to stop trying."

"No one on the surface is going to submit to that, ever," Scout said. "They think of that planet as their own. They resent sending the bulk of the harvests up here already. Once they find out about the inflated numbers, there really will be mutiny. Plus, the only good they see coming from up here is the magnetic shield. Once they know you're dismantling that..." Scout broke off with a shrug.

"They must suspect already," Emilie said. "They're building a gun large enough to destroy *Amatheon Orbiter 1* with a single shot."

"All we have is information," Scout said. "Information everyone already knows or suspects. I don't see how we can do anything at all. But Liam can. Can you help me find him?"

"I don't know what more we can do than what Sergeant Murray is already doing," Seeta said. "Geeta knows more. When she's home again, we can ask her."

"There might be more people in Galactic Central that would help us than just the people your friend knows," Emilie said. "If we could get this information out past the barricade, maybe?"

"This barricade," Scout prompted.

"It's confusing," Seeta said. "We don't really understand what's going on. It has something to do with the Tajaki trade dynasty. We've searched all the databases—"

"Even the secret ones no one is supposed to know about," Emilie put in.

"—but we can't get a sense of the bigger picture," Seeta finished. "The Tajaki trade dynasty sent our ancestors out here to exploit this planet, and when we receive shipments from the surface, agricultural or mining goods or whatever, we load them up into unmanned capsules that get sent back to Galactic Central. No one from the Tajaki trade dynasty has ever come here since the colony was founded. We don't even have any way to verify if anyone is even picking up the capsules."

"That changed a few years ago," Emilie said. "After the war, but not right after. We keep debating whether that's a cause-and-effect thing or not, but we just can't tell."

"The Tajaki trade dynasty put up the barricade?" Scout asked.

"That's the thing," Emilie said. "Near as we can tell, the barricade is there to keep them *out*. And yet they own this planet. I've hacked into everything. Seeta has talked with people very familiar with upper management, but no one seems to know who they are or why they are sealing us off from the rest of the galaxy."

"I think Liam knows," Scout said. "He didn't say anything to me. We were only together for a matter of minutes before he was taken, but I got the sense that he knew. Certainly, he knew he was breaking laws by evading the barricade."

"There are others who might know as well," Seeta said. "I've been making friends with people in the counterculture. Some of them know black marketers, illegal traders from Galactic Central or other not-here places. But they are slow to trust others. I know there is a secret market where they gather and trade, but it is hidden and maybe even mobile. I hear lots of stories. The counterculture kids are all about disrupting the norms, but the traders are just here to make some money. They don't like to talk politics or take sides or do anything that might affect their ability to trade here, but surely they know something about the family dynasties that dominate the legal trade system. Maybe even something that can help us."

"It's a long process," Emilie said, clearly trying to sound supportive but not quite hiding her frustration. "If you're too pushy too fast, they get suspicious and they're gone."

"I'm getting close," Seeta said. "I might have an in."

"So we just wait?" Scout asked, frustrated herself. "Wait for you to make inroads? Wait for Sergeant Murray to find Liam? Do you have any idea who even took him?" Then a horrible thought struck her. "It wasn't Planet Dwellers, was it?" she asked.

"No," Emilie said. "The people in black not-quite-uniforms. No one knows who they are, but they definitely aren't from the Enclave, or from upper management."

"How do you know?" Scout asked.

"Nothing official, just things we've heard," Emilie said. "But the common thread never changes. Everyone is afraid of them. They appear and disappear out of nowhere, giving mysterious commands that are always obeyed. Both the Enclave and upper management have reversed decisions they never would have reversed in normal circumstances, changing their position after encountering one of the people in black."

"So, are they from the Tajaki family dynasty? Or whoever erected the barricade?" Scout asked.

"If we knew that, we might just know what's actually going on," Seeta said.

Emilie nodded, then reached for more butter chicken.

15

AFTER THE DISHES were cleaned up and put away, the heating ring and rice cooker stowed, the table wiped down, and the benches folded back up into the walls, Seeta tapped open four long, rectangular compartments. Bunks, two on each side of the room. They had more little cabinets inside and little personal touches that made it easy to guess who slept where.

Seeta's bunk had a lovely handmade afghan folded neatly at the foot of it and a little ledge the perfect size to hold a mug of tea near the pile of decorative pillows at the head of the bunk. A reader had been left out on the bedspread, half tucked under the pillows.

Over her bunk was her sister's, just as neat if more utilitarian. A stack of folded laundry, all navy-blue jumpsuits, was waiting for her at the foot of the bed.

Emilie had removed the doors from all of her little compartments, a range of electronic devices and random tools packed into each in full view and easy reach. She kicked off her shoes and climbed on top of the unmade bunk.

The bunk over Emilie's looked like they used it for storage: a basket of yarn scraps, an oversized cooking pot that wouldn't fit in the kitchen cabinet, a folding rack Scout had no clue to the use of, and a truly frightening number of scarves from sheer to bulky in all lengths and colors. Seeta gathered it all up and piled it onto the table until the neatly made bed finally came into view.

"You can get water from the sink," Seeta said as she smoothed out the bedcover. "The shower and toilet share the space behind this door here," she said, opening a very narrow doorway next to the sink. "It's not roomy, but at least it's private. The lower levels share communal bathrooms, which are bigger—they even have bathtubs down there—but no privacy. Lucky for us, we got this apartment in the lottery when we left the dorms, otherwise I don't know how we would be able to hide you."

"Thank you," Scout said, climbing up into the bunk. "For everything."

"Tomorrow will be better," Seeta promised her. "We'll figure out what to do, I'm sure."

Scout gave her a stiff smile. She didn't feel so confident about anything.

Seeta did a last few tidying-up chores, then climbed into her own bunk and, after murmuring a soft good night to the others, closed her bunk door. Beneath Scout, Emilie was working on something. Scout could hear the soft clink of tools knocking against each other, punctuated from time to time by Emilie muttering to herself under her breath. The light from her bunk spilled across the apartment floor, glinting a bit too brightly off the stainless-steel table.

Scout found the handle to swing her own bunk door closed and tried not to imagine that she was trapped inside a coffin.

Back home she usually slept out in the open, under the stars in a bedroll spread over a nest of grass. But being in a confined space wasn't what was keeping her from getting comfortable.

She hadn't spent a night alone since she had gotten Shadow, nearly a year before her family had died. Shadow had always been her constant companion, following her everywhere all during the day and at night, insisting she hold him in her arms. When he was a puppy with sharp puppy teeth, he used to scratch up her wrists, pulling at her sleeves until she took the hint.

She missed his warmth, the soft sound of his breathing, the weight of his head on her biceps. Her arms felt weird, like they didn't know how to lie without the dog to define their position.

Gert wasn't as cuddly as Shadow, but she took up twice the space. She liked to curl up behind Scout's knees, occasionally resting her head on Scout's hip if she needed to stare at Scout for whatever reason. That was usually how Scout woke up in the morning, to the persistent feeling of a big black dog watching her closely, waiting for her eyes to open.

Scout clutched the pillow tighter. She was exhausted, she needed the sleep, but her heart was breaking. The only upside Scout could see was that her dogs in their medically induced sleep weren't lying awake missing her, too.

It wasn't much comfort.

But eventually she drifted off to a restless sleep.

She woke to the sound of movement outside her bunk. She opened the door and saw the others all awake. Seeta was pouring tea into two tall thermoses. Emilie was eating a bowl of the leftover rice from the night before and tapping from time to time at the side of her glasses.

Geeta was also there, standing next to her bunk as she exchanged the wrinkled jumpsuit she had just slipped out of for one from the stack on her bed.

"Did you sleep at all?" Scout asked.

"No, just stopping in for a change of clothes and a bite of food," Geeta said.

"Aren't you exhausted?"

Geeta looked up at Scout. Her skin had a gray tinge to it and her eyes looked strange, the pupils darting about too quickly. "They gave us stims."

Scout had never had a stim, but to judge by Geeta's appearance, it was infinitely worse than being overly caffeinated. "Maybe I should turn myself in," she said. "You guys know what to do. You don't really need me here to do it."

"No, we do need you," Seeta said. "We need your help."

"We need you not in the Enclave," Emilie said around a mouthful of rice.

"The active search for you is part of the cover Sergeant Murray is using to continue to look for Liam," Geeta said. "The higher-ups think you went to him. If they had you, I'm not sure how she would justify the crew hours keeping up a search with no new leads."

"If you're sure," Scout said.

"I've been through worse," Geeta promised her, although Seeta behind her looked doubtful. But she mustered up a smile before handing one of the thermoses to her sister. Emilie was tucking the other into a shoulder bag.

"Everyone's going to work?" Scout guessed.

"Not me," Seeta said. "I changed shifts with someone. You and I are going to meet up with my potential contact."

"Me?" Scout almost squeaked. "I thought I was supposed to stay in hiding."

Emilie grinned up at her. "Seeta has a plan," she said, but before Scout could press her for an explanation, she and Geeta were gone.

"What's the plan?" Scout asked Seeta. Seeta smiled up at her as she switched on the kettle and took out mugs for tea. Three of them.

"I have a friend coming in a few minutes. He is a wizard. When he's done with you, no one will recognize you from the images from yesterday."

"What's he going to do?" Scout asked nervously.

"Don't worry, you'll love it," Seeta said. "It looks like Emilie ate all the rice. Do you want some toast?"

Scout climbed down from the bunk to take a seat at the table. Seeta put bread into a toaster, turning to look Scout over as she waited for the bread to darken. Her eyes were assessing, and Scout had to remind herself she no longer had a massive lump over her eyebrow deforming her appearance. She looked like her usual self, perfectly ordinary.

But Seeta seemed to be picturing something else.

She had just set the plate of toast in front of Scout, along with a little container of nut butter, when a chime echoed through the small room.

"That's Rudolf," Seeta said, sliding around the table to open the door. Her body blocked Scout's view of the hallway, although Scout suspected Seeta's intent had actually been the opposite: to keep anyone in the hallway from seeing Scout. Seeta caught both of Rudolf's hands and pulled him into the apartment, shutting the door before pulling him closer to air-kiss each of his cheeks.

"Ah, you've made your very lovely tea," Rudolf said with warm appreciation, setting an overly stuffed bag on the table before sitting down across from Scout. "Hello," he said, smiling at Scout.

He was very pale, as most Space Farers were to Scout's eyes, with hair not so much candy red as a deep crimson that shot straight up from the top of his head to fall in a cascade that framed the left side of his face. He had silver lines in a filigree pattern traced around his right eye and jewelry on his hands that were both rings and bracelets at once in a complicated pattern of chains that clinked together as he sipped at his tea.

Surely she was looking at the counterculture.

Scout focused on her toast. Plain, ordinary toast spread with nut butter. It perfectly suited her.

What were they planning to do with her?

"Her hair is such a lovely shade," Rudolf said to Seeta.

"I know, isn't it?" Seeta agreed. "Now, Emilie has given her a headband that flares on camera, so we just need to make her less recognizable to human eyes."

"Nothing too drastic?" Rudolf said, really a question as he raised his eyebrows to Scout.

"I don't know, I guess," Scout mumbled.

"Don't worry," Rudolf said, squeezing her hand. "You're going to love it. That's always my guarantee. And nothing is permanent. I'd like to start with a hair treatment and then a cut before we decide what we want to do with the color." He got up and moved around the table to stand over her. "May I?"

Scout nodded, and then his fingers were in her hair, stroking the length of it. He made a tsking sound. "Something bad?" Scout asked.

"I've never seen damage like this," Rudolf said.

"She's from the surface," Seeta said in Scout's defense.

"Ah, yes. Sun and wind," Rudolf said, then leaned down to see Scout's face. "Maybe salt water too?"

"No," Scout said. "I didn't live near an ocean."

"And you cut this yourself," Rudolf said, examining the ends of her hair.

"It gets in the way," Scout said.

"Well. How about we get it all out of the way?" Rudolf said with a grin.

"All?" Scout gulped, but Rudolf had gone back around the table to pull a tiny tablet the size of his palm out of his bag. He tapped at it, frowning as he swiped past several things Scout couldn't see before finally breaking into a wide grin.

"Yes, this," he said. Seeta peered over his shoulder.

"With her face shape? Absolutely lovely," Seeta agreed.

Rudolf smiled indulgently at Scout, then turned the tablet around so she could see. It was a picture of a girl with hair cut so short but sleek it looked like she was wearing a cap that came down low on her forehead.

"I'm thinking just a touch of orange," Rudolf said, Seeta nodding along. "It will bring out a different spectrum of your own color, not too drastic, but with the cut, you'll be unrecognizable."

"But pretty," Seeta interjected.

Scout had never once in her life given any thought to whether she was pretty or not. She liked the color of her hair because it reminded her of her mother, but Rudolf had said the change wouldn't be permanent.

"Okay," Scout said, struggling to summon up a smile.

If all this meant she could travel through the city without riding on the back of trains or running up twenty-four flights of stairs, it would be worth it.

16

SCOUT WASN'T USED to strangers touching her this much. It was awkward at first, but after Rudolf gently teased her for flinching, she forced herself to relax. By the time he was done with the conditioning treatment, she really was relaxed. Having someone else gently holding her head under the sink, rinsing the bubbles away, was kind of comforting. That and the warmth of the water; Scout bathed outdoors using water from a spigot when she managed to bathe at all. She had always appreciated the decadence of hot water and soap, but now she was discovering there were more layers.

Watching all the curls of hair falling to the floor around her as Rudolf cut first with scissors and then with an electric trimmer was a bit disconcerting. She became aware of the cool air of the room on her scalp, especially near the back of her neck where he had shaved it almost smooth. But Rudolf and Seeta kept up a light banter, Seeta digging through Rudolf's bag and trying things on herself as Rudolf worked on Scout.

By lunchtime, he had finished. Scout had been afraid she was going to look like she had a pumpkin shell on her head, but the product that had looked vivid orange on his hands before he rubbed it in was having a much subtler effect, shifting honey blonde to something more like a ginger blond.

And there was no way the wind was going to blow her hair into her eyes. She could get used to that.

Seeta had added a long purple streak to her black hair, flowing past her ear to wind its way through her long plait. She had also stenciled a small black filigree pattern over the ends of her eyebrows, a subtler effect than Rudolf's more elaborate silver work. Scout thought it suited her.

"Off to meet your fellow?" Rudolf asked as he packed up his bag. Seeta flushed deeply.

"I thought we were meeting your contact," Scout said.

"Yes," Seeta mumbled.

"Now listen, Seeta," Rudolf said in mock sternness. "Take care of your heart. Those foreign boys are all trouble."

"This is business," Seeta said. "Just business."

Rudolf didn't look like he believed that for a minute, but he let it go. "How about you?" he asked Scout. "Happy with your look?"

"Yes, it's very interesting," Scout said. He laughed.

"It's a big change for you; shock is normal. Come find me again in a few weeks and we'll see what we can do to really change it up." He winked at her before leaving the apartment.

"So, you like this guy we're going to meet?" Scout asked.

"It's not like that," Seeta said. "It's a game, a flirting game. This is how I get in. I cultivate relationships. This guy knows where the secret black marketplace is, and he's been promising to take me there. Where we're going now has some black-market stuff, but it's just special food and clothes. Nothing too objectionable, so management lets it go. But the secret black marketplace has more stuff. Dogs, like I mentioned to you before. Drugs. Weapons."

"And we have to go there because…?"

"That's where the real foreigners hide from the management. The ones who can tell us things. Maybe even get you out of here if we end up not able to find your friend. But they won't come out to talk to us, so we have to get in to talk to them."

"I don't know, it sounds dangerous," Scout said.

"Says the girl who nearly fell the length of a tower yesterday," Seeta said.

She gave Scout a spare jumpsuit—one of hers, as it was purple—but Scout kept the sneakers Emilie had given her, as well as the scarf with all the shades of blue. Anything to temper the clash between the purple of her suit and the orange of her hair. Seeta shook out a long rectangle of silky lavender fabric and threw it over one shoulder, tying the ends loosely at the opposite waist, and slipped her feet into brightly white canvas shoes.

"Let me check first," Seeta said, hand on the door. "Your disguise is good, but it's probably better if none of the neighbors sees you. They'll know you're not Geeta or Emilie."

"Got it," Scout said, staying clear of the doorway until Seeta gave her the nod.

They passed no one in the hallway, but when the elevator arrived, there was already a man on it. Scout tensed, preparing to run, but Seeta took her hand and gave it a reassuring squeeze.

Scout followed her into the elevator, trying to take in the details of the man's appearance without getting caught staring. Like Sergeant Murray, he was wearing a uniform of a nicer fabric than the ubiquitous jumpsuits. It was even navy blue, like hers. Scout knew the insignia on his chest would indicate his rank, but the tablet he was reading was blocking her view.

He looked old, thinning, steely gray hair cut close to his brown scalp. The way he completely ignored their presence in the shared elevator made Scout think he was probably someone important, or at least he thought he was. And his apartment had been further up the tower than theirs.

The doors opened on the ground floor and Seeta held Scout back until the man had stepped out of the elevator. Then they were heading down the short flight of steps back to the train platform.

"Who was he?" Scout asked the moment they were sitting together in one of the train cars. What a treat to ride *inside* the train.

"I don't know," Seeta admitted. "There are thousands of people in our building. I only know a handful who live on our level."

A few other people boarded their car before the doors closed, but none of them gave Scout and Seeta more than a passing glance. And she could even see herself on a screen at the front of the car. Some camera had caught her walking between Geeta and Sergeant Murray up the steps to the balcony. That had been after her shower, and yet her hair looked matted already. It must have dried in clumps while she was in the medical pod; she hadn't been paying attention.

She touched the back of her neck, her fingertips tickling the short hairs. The ends felt almost sharp.

She could get used to it.

Two stops later, Seeta pulled her to her feet, and they stepped out onto the more crowded train platform under the building with the immense atrium. Scout managed to confine herself to a couple of glances up as they walked under it.

"It is cool," Seeta whispered to her as they walked out the doors. "The station itself is the hull of the ship that brought us here. All the other stations are smaller, built from parts that came out of the center of the ship. That's why the station is hollow in the middle. But the structures here are built out of modular components, kind of like what you have down on the surface but not as durable, since there is no exposure to the elements here. I read they had some sort of design contest and this was one of the winning designs."

"Why towers?" Scout asked.

"That we haven't figured out," Seeta said. They were out on the veranda among the wilted trees. "Emilie says most stations in Galactic Central use mirrors to direct sunlight and let them grow things, so the interiors look like a slice of a planet, with grass and trees and houses. But they didn't do that here. Perhaps the mirrors were damaged. That's what I think."

"Or they didn't want to deal with the coronal mass ejection events," Scout said.

Seeta sucked in her breath. "I bet you're right," she said. "That makes perfect sense."

"So it's always dark here?" Scout asked. How sad. Just spending a couple of days in nothing but artificial light was making her feel listless. Perhaps if you had never been in sunshine you wouldn't miss it? Certainly, no one around her looked as sluggish as Scout felt.

"This is supposed to be a 'sunny zone,'" Seeta said. "Sad, isn't it? There are others, but they are only open to upper management." She slipped her arm through Scout's, leaning in closer to whisper next to her ear as they skirted the fountain. "I've even heard the Board of Three live in a place like Emilie described: a field with grass and trees and their houses all bathed in sunlight. I don't know if it's true, though."

"Where would they hide it?" Scout asked. She had stood on top of two of the towers now. How anyone could hide a thing when anybody could see it from above, she had no idea.

"Inside the towers," Seeta said. "Even before we were orphaned, that was a mystery Emilie was digging into. She had a secret group at school that had a map of the entire station. They were all from other stations, just like Geeta and I, although we weren't so curious then. When we had free time from school, they would explore inside the towers. I guess the first thing they thought was strange was how many weren't open to the general public. Although, frankly, most of those buildings are residences, and why should people be going into towers they don't live in if they aren't invited guests? Emilie was our roommate, but back then we just thought she was weird and maybe too ready to dig into things that were supposed to be off-limits."

"What happened to the group?" Scout asked when Seeta's voice had trailed off.

"Hmm? Oh, it fell apart. Actually, Emilie fell apart the very day we lost our families, and when she finally turned to snooping to deal with her grief, just seeing inside of buildings wasn't what she was looking for anymore. She wanted to know why everything happened and what we could do to stop it from happening again. That's when Geeta and I got on board. We wanted those things too."

"If there is an entire tower that belongs to the Planet Dwellers, maybe there's another one for the people in black?" Scout said.

"Maybe," Seeta said doubtfully. "But everyone knows about the Enclave. If they have their own tower, I don't know how they could be careful enough about coming and going that no one knows they're there."

"Wear jumpsuits, change after they're away from the tower," Scout suggested.

"Maybe."

The crush of people around them was getting too dense for them to carry on such a dangerous conversation, and Scout let it drop.

She had never seen so many shops dedicated to varieties of shoes, caps, and scarves. But it made sense, given that the rest of anyone's look was mandated by their jumpsuits in colors that corresponded to their occupation.

"Through here," Seeta said, catching Scout's hand again. At first she thought Seeta was taking her to one of the shoe shops, but then she saw the narrow gap between the shoe shop and the shop selling candy next to it. They had to turn sideways to sidle through it. Seeta reached her arms high over her head, trying to keep her lavender scarf from brushing up against the not-too-terribly clean walls.

Then they were back out in an open space with shops all around, but these shops were different. No scarves or shoes here; here one could obtain any article of clothing or jewelry or bauble from the far side of the galaxy.

And it smelled amazing. Spices, oil, caramelized sugar, sharp fruity smells she couldn't identify, all blending together in a tantalizing amalgam that had her stomach loudly reminding her all she had eaten that day was toast.

"Come on," Seeta said, taking her by the arm. "I have to keep an eye out for my contact, but he might not approach me if I'm not alone. But I know just the place for you to wait for me."

Scout almost yelped in protest. There was so much around her she wanted to take a closer look at, to touch and smell and maybe taste. But when Seeta finally let go of her hand, Scout had to admit she had taken Scout somewhere pretty cool.

An entire shop selling nothing but jolo.

But wait. The labels varied, a rainbow of colors.

Jolo came in flavors?

Seeta was beaming at her. "No one will know it's you if you look like you're enjoying yourself, right? This should buy you a couple to try," she said, pressing a plastic coin into Scout's hand. "Choose wisely."

Scout let several groups of schoolkids go first to give her time. Some of the flavors didn't even mean anything to her—galactic fruits that had never been introduced on Amatheon, she was guessing—and others didn't seem like a good combination with jolo at all. Black pepper? Hot sauce? Really?

She was halfway through a bottle of lemon jolo, the sugar and caffeine making her brain sing as always, when she saw Seeta now had someone strolling around the market with her. But it wasn't a boy. It was a girl of maybe ten, thin, with dark skin and hair arranged in an impressive globe atop her head. Was this the contact or some random stranger?

Scout watched Seeta talk with the girl as she sipped at the second bottle, a rich cherry flavor. Almost too rich, but she liked it.

And all of this came from Galactic Central. So much awaited her there. She just needed to get Liam back first.

Seeta came skipping back to her and Scout handed her the half-finished lemon jolo. Seeta took a sip.

"Well?" Scout prompted.

"I'm in," Seeta said. "We're in. Hal's meeting us tonight. That was his sister. She's been here watching for me all day because he was super anxious to get word to me." She sipped again and gave Scout a smile that, for once, didn't look genuine. "He wanted to come himself, but his sister said it wasn't safe for him to come out of the black market. She wouldn't say why, not here with so many people around, but I think I know why. I've been asking him lots of questions about the people in black, and I think he knows more than he says about who they are, where they come from, what they're up to. But his sister was implying that something major has happened just since yesterday, and I think I know what she was hinting at and why Hal is hiding. I think he knows where Liam is."

She took another long pull from the bottle, somehow managing to keep smiling at Scout while she drank. Scout felt dizzy from all the jolo but smiled back. Just a normal girl hanging with her friend, drinking fizzy drinks together. Definitely not the girl who was thrown off a walkway the day before.

If things worked out, she would be back with Liam before midnight and they'd be out of here. How could she squash even a flicker of hope?

Scout drained the last of the cherry jolo and smiled at the world around her. Back with Liam, and then back with her dogs. She wouldn't have to sleep alone for even one more night.

17

A FEW HOURS LATER, they met Geeta and Emilie on the train platform near the marketplace. Seeta herded them all into a train car, but it was too crowded for them to talk without risk of being overheard. There was only one open seat and Geeta took it, rolling her head back against the wall of the train car. She was asleep before the train even started moving.

"Are you sure she's okay?" Scout asked. Geeta looked paler than ever, except for the darkening patches under her eyes.

"This is nearly over," Seeta said, but Scout could see she was worried by the way she furrowed her brows.

"She's got extra stims on her if she needs them," Emilie said. "But it's good that she's napping now, while she can. How far are we going?"

"End of the line," Seeta said. "Maybe twenty minutes?"

"How long can she keep taking stims?" Scout asked.

"Do you see the band on her wrist?" Emilie asked. Scout nodded. "That's her security communicator, but it also continuously monitors her vitals. If she starts falling out of acceptable parameters, she'll be pulled from duty and required to rest."

"The ones who run into trouble are upper management who don't answer to anyone and ignore their own readings. But that doesn't come up too much," Seeta said.

"Not since the war," Emilie said. "Officers routinely worked until they collapsed then."

Scout saw the screen in the front of the train car displaying her image again, but no one around her looked her way. Her disguise was working. She glanced up at her reflection in the window behind Geeta. She scarcely recognized herself.

Were her dogs going to know her?

As they continued down the line, more people were exiting the train than boarding and soon there were chairs enough for all of them. Emilie slouched down in hers, tapping her glasses from time to time. Seeta was fussing with the hem of her lavender scarf, smoothing it out against her thigh over and over.

The view outside the train windows was a blur of passing walls, all the same dull gray. The train platforms were more interesting. Scout tried to get a sense as to the neighborhoods above by what was going on below. One platform had walls painted with a vivid mural, some fantastical world with magical creatures and glittering palaces. The art district, or maybe a theater district? Another platform was swarming with children and Scout guessed they must be near a school, perhaps the one the other three had attended once upon a time.

The last platform was empty of people, the walls unmarked.

"End of the line," said a voice from a speaker near the display screen. Seeta shook Geeta awake, and they got down from the train. A few other people exited the other cars and headed for the stairs up to street level without so much as a glance to the four girls standing together.

"Where to now?" Scout asked.

"Wait for the train to head back," Seeta said. "Pretend like we're consulting something."

Geeta yawned as she looked at her wrist communicator. The notification light was actually flashing, but she dismissed it with a touch.

At last the train pulled away, back the way it had come, and they were alone.

"Okay, this way," Seeta said, going to the edge of the platform and stepping down to the walkway that ran the length of the tunnel. The tunnel ended only one train car's length away.

"There's nothing here," Scout said, but then someone stepped out of the shadows at the very end of the tunnel.

"End of the line," he said, walking toward them with his hands near his hips in a position Scout knew all too well. That was how Gertrude Bauer had always stood, ready to draw and fire her weapon in the blink of an eye. The fact that Scout couldn't see a weapon around his waist didn't comfort her much. Someone who concealed his weapons was certainly more dangerous.

"The end of one line is the beginning of another," Seeta said, her voice lifting up at the end as if asking the man if her words were correct. He looked her over, then Scout and Emilie, but he stopped at Geeta's navy-blue jumpsuit.

"You three look all right," he said. "But I don't think we need security here. Not even ensigns."

"I didn't have time to change," Geeta said, her voice almost gravelly with exhaustion. She unfastened the front of her jumpsuit and rolled it down to tie it by the sleeves around her waist. The tank top she wore underneath had tiny lights worked into the design, lights that changed color in a slow swirl that was almost hypnotic.

Then she reached up and unpinned her hair, letting the braid cascade down. Then she unplaited it and bent forward to shake out her loose hair. She pulled it into a topknot, then straightened back up.

The back of her hair was a bright pink with a strand running through it, much like Seeta's purple lock.

"You can go ahead," the man said. "But I've got my eye on you."

"Thank you," Seeta said, but he just waved them past. At the point where he had emerged from the darkness, a doorway lurked, all but invisible in the shadows so far from the light from the platform. Seeta pulled it open, then led the way down a long, narrow staircase.

"The color in your hair means something?" Scout asked Geeta.

"It's a counterculture thing. That's why he let me through. Management tolerates it to some extent, especially if you're otherwise brilliant at your work like Emilie here. But it would be strictly forbidden for me in security," Geeta explained.

"How do you keep it all hidden when it's on the back of your head?" Scout asked.

"Seeta does it for me," Geeta said.

Sounds were drifting up toward them, people talking and laughing and music playing. Still, the narrow staircase kept going down, ever deeper. Just how far below the train level were they?

"Is this the sublevel?" Scout asked.

"The sublevels are a labyrinth," Emilie said. "Some sections connect, others don't. I've been down in them a few times, enough to know that a lot of changes were made that weren't updated on the official schematics."

"That's why it's been so hard to find your friend," Geeta said. "But it's also why a place like this can exist."

Scout was about to ask what sort of place it was when suddenly they were at the bottom of the stairs and then out on a catwalk and she could see for herself. She supposed in the schematics this was an open space between two massive bulkheads. Although she could not detect a curve to the floor, she was certain they had gone as far down as it was possible to go: all the way down to the outer shell of the station cylinder, what remained of the hull of the original freighter.

But the open space was far from empty. The catwalk extended down the middle of the space, but all around it—to both sides, as well as above and below—were structures built from the usual snap-together components. Scout guessed these pieces had been the left-overs, a lot of irregular shapes or damaged pieces, but still usable for defining a space if you were creative. There were structures suspended from the ceiling high above, delicate as birdcages and only reachable by a dangling ladder. Looking through the grate of the catwalk gave glimpses into the roofless buildings below, the people carousing together in the bars or negotiating in the shops.

Scout guessed you could buy anything in the galaxy here. She saw equipment much like Gertrude's, delicate electronics that functioned only in conjunction with some sort of eyewear. Gertrude had worn mirrored lenses, but glasses like Emilie's were an option too, apparently.

They passed a tiny space where two people in long white coats were injecting a needle into someone reclining in a chair. Nanites? Scout wanted to double back and ask, but Seeta was setting too brisk a pace.

A few people around her wore the usual jumpsuits, but most had found little ways to modify them: removing sleeves or adding scarves. Scout supposed they all had to be able to blend back in when they went back upstairs.

Everyone had some bright color to their hair. Patches that could be carefully hidden away were common, but others had gone all in like Emilie. The bright colors and loud music that had people everywhere dancing gave the place an air of jubilation that Scout hadn't been expecting from a black market.

"I think this is it," Seeta said, guiding them off the sturdy catwalk and into a swaying rope bridge that curved up and up to a cluster of structures built high against one of the bulkheads. They left the music behind, although the deep thumping bass could still be heard and felt.

The bridge ended in a doorway, the interior of the structure dark compared to the neon brightness of the rest of the market. They had to stop just a few steps in and let their eyes adjust.

As the room came into detail around her, it reminded Scout of the public houses back on Amatheon. It offered food and drink, but was primarily a place for people to meet and talk. People leaned close together around tables and in booths, speaking earnestly and low. This wasn't a place for parties; business was being conducted.

There was less of the candy-colored hair here, and fewer jumpsuits. Most of the people gathered here wore drab colors, work clothes more of the sort Scout was used to, clothes to get dirty in. Which wasn't to say they were cheap, they just weren't flashy.

These were galactic people. Traders. Black marketers. And somewhere among them was Seeta's contact.

18

GEETA WAS SCANNING the room with slow deliberation, not looking the patrons in their faces but observing every detail of the space. Scout followed her gaze, noting the balcony that overlooked the main room, the empty booth in the corner farthest from that balcony, a table just being abandoned by a pair of traders.

"Did he want to meet you alone?" Scout asked, remembering that morning in the marketplace.

"I think so," Seeta said. She also was looking around the room with a small frown. "I don't see him."

"He'll come to you," Geeta guessed. "Take a seat in that booth with your back to the balcony. I want to see him when he sits across from you. Emilie, sit at that table with your back to Seeta and keep watching the room, especially in the corners I won't be able to see. Scout, you're coming with me up to the balcony."

"What if he's already here and saw us come in together?" Scout asked.

"He isn't here," Seeta said.

"Let's go," Geeta said, and they all headed to their respective spaces.

The stairs up to the balcony had a sway to them that made Scout a bit nervous, but it was only half a level up, so if it collapsed, she wouldn't get hurt too badly. What had appeared to be a railing from below was actually a narrow bar with stools tucked under it. Geeta grabbed a bowl of nuts from an empty table and set it between two stools at the point of the balcony that gave them the best view of Seeta sitting alone in her booth, twisting her hair nervously as she waited.

"Have you ever met Hal?" Scout asked.

"Not up close," Geeta said, pausing her methodical shoveling of nut after nut into her mouth. "Seeta met him at a counterculture party we were all at, but she was across the room from me when she was chatting him up."

"But you know what he looks like?"

Geeta nodded, mouth too full to speak. She swallowed. "Sorry. Stims make me crazy hungry."

"Do you want me to go down and order you something to eat?" Scout asked, assuming because it looked like a public house back on Amatheon that the service worked the same.

"Not now," Geeta said, sitting up straighter. "He's here."

Scout leaned forward on her elbows, trying to look like she was casually surveying the scene, not letting her gaze linger too long on the tall, lanky youth slinking in the doorway. His hair was twisted in tight coils close to his scalp, only the very ends of the coils dyed a rich red. The hair might say counterculture, but the clothes were all foreign: jeans, an intensely white T-shirt, and a leather vest. They were good quality, Scout could tell even from a glance at a distance. They had that simple elegance she associated with clothes from Galactic Central.

"Is he from here or not?" Scout asked.

"Shh," Geeta hissed, setting a small black disk on the bar between them. Scout stared at it, completely baffled until she heard Seeta's voice trickling up through it.

"Hal! I was getting worried." There was a rustle, and Scout looked up to see Seeta standing to greet her friend with a hug. The sound coming from the disk was muffled and Scout realized it must be connected to something Seeta was wearing, hidden.

Hal hugged her back, and they started to pull away when he tugged her close again and kissed her full on the mouth.

Geeta scowled.

"Wow. What was that for?" Seeta asked.

"If you knew what my life has been like since yesterday," he said, rubbing at the back of his neck as if he could feel them watching him. Then he turned to look around the room.

Geeta's hand closed on Scout's wrist, silently telling her not to quickly turn her head the way she had just been about to. Instead, Scout shifted her gaze to Emilie. Emilie was tapping her hands against the table and bobbing to her own beat. In short, providing a perfectly logical thing for anyone to be watching rather than the couple meeting surreptitiously behind her.

Hal finished his perusal of the room and released Seeta. They slid into the booth. Hal's eyes scanned across the balcony again, passing over Geeta and Scout without pausing, then shifted down to focus on Seeta. "I've been in a 'do it now for tomorrow you may die' kind of place since yesterday. Sorry if I overstepped."

"It's all right," Seeta said, still sounding flustered. "What's going on? Are you okay? Your sister sounded worried about you."

"She's right to be," Hal said, leaning forward and lowering his voice. "Look, I've been digging into anything anybody knows about the people in black not-uniforms since we met, right? But I've always come up empty. If word ever got back around to them that I was hunting for info, they didn't seem to care. And why should they? I had nothing."

"You said you thought your bosses knew who these people are," Seeta said.

"I still think they do, but they aren't saying. Not to me. When I ask, they tell me to focus on my work. One of them even said that I'm 'not there yet.' They know, and with time, they might even trust me enough to tell me. But now there is no time."

He caught one of her hands in his, twining their fingers together. His eyes kept darting around, but Scout suspected this was only half a diversion made to look like they were having an ordinary conversation. He looked scared and in need of a comforting touch.

"So all of this stuff was just lurking under the surface, dormant, and my bosses weren't even pretending it wasn't there. But then you asked me to dig into that abduction."

"You've got something?" Seeta asked. Scout could see her back straighten.

"No," Hal said, and Seeta's shoulders slumped. Scout's heart sank even lower. "Nothing but trouble. Well, maybe a lead, I don't know."

Seeta leaned in, bringing her other hand up to clutch at his. "Tell me."

"You said you thought they had gone to sublevel 85-GG, right? I have a friend who works maintenance near there. He also does some side business with my bosses, not as much as me, but he's in the game. So I asked, and he said yeah. The security details had been combing that area, but he knew they weren't going to find anything. The black market used to be there, but not lately. They must have been following up old rumors or old actual info or whatever, but like I said, old. Nothing there anymore. So I told him if someone had disappeared near there, where would they likely be? And he said he had some thoughts and would get back to me."

"Okay," Seeta said. "And when he got back to you?"

"That's just it," Hal said. "He died. Accident on the job. Electrocution. Not three minutes after he finished talking to me. Somebody was listening, somebody heard, and somebody eliminated him."

"And now they're after you?"

"They're definitely after me," Hal said. "I was going about my usual business, hopping from train platform to train platform and meeting folks looking to buy what I was carrying. If I had a sit-in-one-place kind of job, they would have eliminated me already. And I heard about the accident before I was meant to go home for the day, so I just kept moving instead. And soon as I could, I came down here. Only I don't know if here is even safe."

"Who's trying to kill you? The people in black or your bosses?" Seeta asked.

"I don't know," Hal said, chewing at the side of his thumb. "I'm so afraid it's maybe both. I haven't even tried to contact my bosses. I mean, I spoke to one briefly early in the day yesterday when it was still business as usual. She sounded normal, but who knows?"

"So we still don't know who the people in black are or what they're up to or where they took the marshal," Seeta said.

"I know they're dangerous," Hal said. "I sent my sister to tell you to meet me here because I didn't think you'd take her seriously if I told her to tell you to run. But I really think you should run."

"Run where?" Seeta asked.

"Anywhere," Hal said. "I'm trying to get my sister and I off this station. She's searching for a pilot and a ship right now. One with no ties to either the people in black or my bosses. She's been down here since she met with you." He broke off, pulling his hands free to rub at the back of his neck again. "I feel like I'm being watched. All the time like I'm being watched. I wanted to come to you yesterday, but I was so sure they were watching me and following me because they wanted me to lead them to you. I really don't know if we're even safe here anymore."

"I can get us all off this station," Seeta said, "but I need to find that man first. Your friend didn't give you any idea what he was thinking before he died?"

"No," Hal said. "He said he had three possibilities, but he wanted to check some things."

"You should go to your sister, lie low," Seeta said. "I have friends who can investigate from here. You've done enough. More than enough."

"Maybe too much," Hal said with a humorless laugh, but then he caught her hand again in a tight squeeze. "We'll all leave here? Together?"

"I promise," Seeta said. "Once we have the marshal back, everything is going to be fine."

"And if he's dead already?" Hal asked.

Scout bit her lip. She had been avoiding asking herself that very question for some time now. How long would his captors hold him? If they were going to let him go, it seemed like they would have done it already. The only hope to hold on to was that they needed him, perhaps as a hostage to some other entity.

The last thing they needed was another player in the game to keep track of. She could hardly keep track of all the conflicting motivations they were already trying to navigate through.

"One thing at a time," Seeta said in that quietly confident way she had. "First thing is to get you somewhere safer. Where is your sister now?"

Hal flinched suddenly, slapping at the side of his neck. He opened his mouth to answer Seeta, but all that came out was a gurgle. Scout saw his hands on Seeta's clutching tighter, painfully tighter, to judge by Seeta's hiss of breath. Then Seeta cried out, lunging to her feet to catch Hal's head in her hands.

He was sliding out of his seat, down and sideways, his head lolling. Seeta turned his face up to look at him and Scout saw bloody froth escaping from his lips, his eyes locked on hers. He was trying to form words as Seeta, weeping, touched his face.

Then her fingers moved down his neck. Scout knew what Seeta would find: nothing. The assassins she had tangled with before had killed from afar, and their weapons had left no mark save a small red dot like an insect sting.

Only there were no insects here.

19

HER OWN BREATHING sounded too loud in Scout's ears. All the other sounds in the public house around her were still there but were muted, like her head was underwater. She couldn't move, not even to brush aside the tickle of tears streaming down her face.

To think she had enough fingers to count back the days to a point where she had never seen a dead body. And not enough fingers to count all the ones she'd seen since.

She had never even properly met Hal, and it sounded like whatever he did for his bosses was at least partially unsavory, but Seeta moaning his name over and over again was more than Scout could bear.

She blinked once, hard, and stopped the tears. Then she uprooted her feet from the floor to run to Seeta.

Emilie had jumped to her feet, knocking her chair to the floor behind her and pointing to a position behind and to the left of Scout. Scout looked back and saw Geeta already charging in that direction, something metallic gleaming in her hand.

Someone else was fleeing from Geeta, knocking chairs and tables over to slow her down. Scout couldn't get a close enough look to see any identifying features, only a swirl of cloak and a glimpse of pants that looked like they were real leather.

Cloak and pants both a deep inky black. It was like they pulled shadows behind her to cover her retreat.

Seeta had lowered Hal to the floor and was clutching his hand. He was still laboring to speak, and she leaned down, putting her ear close to his blood-flecked lips. Scout reached her side and stood behind her, putting a comforting hand on her shoulder.

"Can we move him?" Emilie asked. She had backed up to stand beside them but was still facing the other way. Geeta had disappeared.

The other clientele in the public house were starting to notice that something was going on. Some willfully ignored it and just carried on with their conversations, but others were melting away.

No one was coming over to help.

"He's gone," Seeta said. She gently laid his hand down on his chest, picking up the other to put it on top. The pain had gone from his face. He looked restful.

"We should be gone too," Emilie said.

"Geeta?" Scout asked.

"She went out the back. Come on," Emilie said, leading the way back up the stairs. Scout helped Seeta to her feet. She was worried that Seeta would be distraught, maybe not want to leave her friend's side, but there was none of that on Seeta's face, just a grim determination. They paused at the top of the stairs only long enough for Scout to retrieve the little disk and put it in her pocket.

They followed the trail of overturned chairs to another even narrower flight of steps. This led to a veranda on top of the building overlooking the entire black market. Geeta was there, standing at the very edge and staring down into the market below.

"She got away," Geeta said. "She just jumped. She must have had a line or something waiting as an escape route."

The four of them stood at the edge for several minutes, eyes sweeping the market below them for any sign of a black cloak or a person moving more swiftly than the others, but there was no sign of their quarry.

"Now what?" Scout asked.

"We should get back to the apartment," Geeta said.

"Is it safe?" Scout asked.

"Maybe nowhere is," Seeta said.

"It's safe enough," Emilie said. "My equipment is there. I need it."

"Did Hal give you enough to go on?" Seeta asked hopefully. "He never said his friend's name or what he was digging into."

"I think I have enough," Emilie said. "I don't need his name. How many people do you think died from electrocution yesterday? I'll find his name, and his workstation, and his computer system access history. Even if he was careful, I'll know everything by tomorrow morning. But we have to get back to the apartment."

"His sister…" Seeta said, but she shook her head. "I don't have any way of getting a message to her."

"Hal was smart, and he was worried," Geeta said, giving her sister's arm a tight squeeze. "He would have planned for this. She will know when he doesn't return that he's likely dead. He surely gave her a deadline; if he's not back then, she bugs out on her own."

"That sounds like Hal," Seeta agreed. "But how scary for her, to be on her own at such an age."

They all exchanged uncomfortable glances. They had all lost their own families at nearly the same age and managed okay, but it wasn't a fate any of them would wish on anyone.

"There's another way back," Emilie said, pointing to a rickety walkway that clung to the edge of the bulkhead, leading from the veranda to the far wall of the space. Geeta led the way, keeping her sister close beside her. Emilie herded Scout ahead of her so she could bring up the rear.

The merry sounds of the marketplace grew louder as they approached the far wall, but they sounded like a mockery now. The laughter was a touch too loud, the music too aggressively upbeat. It felt like a desperate attempt at a party, as if everyone below knew the war was coming and it couldn't be stopped. As if they all shared Hal's 'do it now for tomorrow, you may die' philosophy. But it wasn't making anyone happy.

It was a relief to leave all of that behind them as they climbed the long set of stairs back up to the train tunnel. The guard was leaning against the wall with his arms crossed, half in the shadows, but watched them leave without a word.

They climbed back up to the train platform and waited. Scout glanced at the chronometer on Geeta's wrist comm. It wasn't even bedtime yet.

"He told me something, just before he died," Seeta said. She was whispering, although there was no one else waiting on the platform with them.

"What did he say?" Scout asked. They all pressed in close around Seeta.

"He said his bosses worked for the Tajaki dynasty."

"That doesn't make any sense," Scout said. "Why would the Tajaki dynasty be running black market trade into their own station?"

"The barricade," Emilie said. "Remember, it's not theirs. It's to keep them out."

"Still, once they're past it, why not just trade openly with your... management?" Scout asked.

"They can't," Geeta said. They waited for her to say more, but she just looked thoughtful.

"Management knows the black market is there. It tolerates it," Emilie said, thinking out loud.

"But it can't publicly acknowledge it," Geeta said, also thinking it through. "But the Tajaki dynasty is technically their bosses, so if they can't acknowledge their own bosses, then someone else is in charge."

"The people in black," Scout said. "They're connected with whoever put up the barricade."

They could hear the sound of the train approaching, growing ever louder as it echoed down the tunnel and around the platform.

"It would be interesting," Geeta said, "to compile every incidence where someone in management reversed a decision after a visit. I know a lot of it is hearsay, but what if we took a look at all of those decisions? Would there be a pattern?"

"Well, that would be interesting, but it's not the first thing I'll be digging into," Emilie said, putting her hands into her pockets as the train stopped beside them. They stepped into a car that had looked empty from the platform, but even though they were at the end of the line, there was still a passenger curled up on one of the seats, fast asleep. Emilie slipped into a chair opposite the sleeper, folding her arms as she prepared to keep an eye on him for the entire journey.

"I won't be going back to the apartment," Geeta said, sliding her arms back into her jumpsuit and covering up the sparkling tank top. "I've delayed reporting back in long enough. I'll be back in the morning for a change of clothes and some breakfast. Overnight oatmeal?"

"I can do that," Seeta said distractedly. She was gazing out the window, watching the platform slide away behind them, her hands folded neatly on her lap. Then she realized her sister was still looking at her and got up to help Geeta turn the multicolored topknot back into the tightly braided conservative do.

"No news on Liam?" Scout asked hopefully as Geeta was once more busy tapping at her comm.

"Nothing," Geeta said. "No leads on you either, so that's good."

"I wish you had gotten a chance to sleep," Scout said.

"I'll be fine," Geeta said. "If there is nothing to follow up on when I get back to the security building, they'll probably have me nap in the back room. It's kind of like being on standby; I'll be right there if something changes."

"If you can sneak a peek at my dogs—"

"I certainly will," Geeta said. "It wouldn't even be suspicious. They are the highlight of security at the moment. Everyone finds an excuse to stop by and watch them. The techs have set up a separate area where they can run around outside of the kennels. It's not a coincidence it's right near the window; they are good for morale. They are still moving a little slow, but they're doing better. Gert is a sweetheart with those big brown eyes, and no matter how groggy she's feeling, that tail just has to wag."

"I was hoping to be back with them before tonight," Scout confessed.

"Soon," Geeta said. "This is my stop. See you all in the morning."

"Good night," Seeta said.

Emilie mumbled a sound that might have been a farewell. Her attention seemed to be divided between something projecting on her glasses and the sleeping passenger across from her, leaving little brain power for social niceties.

Scout watched Geeta disappear into the late evening crowd waiting on the train platform. Everyone in jumpsuits here, no one with brightly colored hair. No one here desperately trying to blot out the fact that they knew bad times were coming.

Didn't they suspect? She saw one couple, laughing together as they looked at a display for some sort of entertainment. They looked like they didn't have a care in the world. And the entertainment—perhaps a video release or a theater production, Scout couldn't really tell— looked bright and garish and, judging from the expression on the actor's face as he mugged at the crowd on the platform, more than a little stupid. No one who knew their time might be tragically short would spend an evening on that.

Soon, they wouldn't be able to ignore it. Soon everyone would know there was an enormous gun already pointed at them. Their lives could be over in a blink.

And over what? Scout knew a long list of grievances dating back to when her ancestors first landed on the planet's surface generations before. But a root cause, an actual reason for all of this, she couldn't even begin to imagine.

So many lives already gone, so many more at stake now. What could possibly be worth all that?

20

SCOUT SPENT A LONG, restless night missing her dogs. She woke several times to find herself reaching around the bed, trying to find the warm body that must have just rolled away, only to come fully awake and remember they weren't there.

She had left her bunk open, as had Seeta, not minding the light from Emilie's bunk or the staccato bursts of tapping as she navigated through the space station's computer systems. Emilie mumbled to herself from time to time, but the shout that Scout and Seeta were both listening for, that she had found something, never came.

Seeta had left the lidded cooker out on the table, and as the night progressed, the smell of slowly cooking oatmeal grew stronger. It permeated what passed for Scout's dreams. It was a comforting smell, but it mixed oddly with the images of every person she had seen die violently before her eyes in the last few days. The faces with their unseeing eyes haunted her.

Scout snapped out of a last light doze at the soft click of Geeta entering the apartment. She had a tote in her arms: Scout's things.

"Morning already?" Seeta asked sleepily as she sat up on one elbow.

"Technically," Geeta said. "It's about two. I was sent home early."

She saw Scout was awake and handed up the tote. Scout took it grate-fully. "The dogs are fine."

"They sent you home because you've had too many stims," Seeta said. Geeta didn't answer.

"We should eat," Emilie said. "We're going to need it."

Without a word, they all climbed out of their bunks and sat down around the table to bowls of oatmeal and more of the milk from the best bio-construct that simulated a cow.

"You found something?" Geeta asked at last.

"I've gone through everything I could find on this friend of Hal's. He's a fellow in his late twenties by the name of Curt Walter. Curt was, not surprisingly, an electrician. I guess the wiring in the station and particularly the sublevels is getting old and prone to issues. Flickering lights, flameouts, stuff like that. He complained about it a lot, but his supervisor couldn't really fix anything. The department didn't have the budget. He started dealing with the black market to get access to equipment he needed just to do his job. I think he was kind of a hero, actually. I'm sorry I didn't get to meet him before he died."

"I'm guessing he didn't know who the people in black not-uniforms worked for," Scout said.

"No, although he was looking into it even before Hal was. And when Hal came to him for help tracking down Liam, he jumped right on it. His own curiosity demanded it. He died before he could figure anything out, but he was on the right track to finding things. I actually narrowed down our possibilities using an algorithm he had been working on, compiling strange sightings or found objects or damage to the station."

"Damage to the station?" Scout asked.

"Signs of gunfights," Emilie clarified. "Although no one specified that in any of their paperwork. Stuff has been going down under our feet for quite some time."

"How much could you narrow down the search?" Scout asked.

"I have three possibilities, but I can't narrow it down any further from here," Emilie said. "We're going to have to go see for ourselves. But I don't think we have much time. We should split up."

"I don't like that idea," Geeta said.

"What are the locations?" Scout asked.

Emilie got up from her chair to dig into the bunk behind her, then set a small spherical object in the center of the table. She tapped her glasses, and the object lit up, projecting a hologram of the entire cylindrical station over the table.

"Not all over the station!" Seeta gasped.

"No, hold on. I'll zoom," Emilie said. The hologram rotated and then zoomed in, wavering lines zipping past their heads before winking out of existence. When she stopped, they were looking at a city grid, blocks of towers plus the trains beneath and deeper levels below the trains.

"All three are in sublevels," Emilie said, "but in different non-connecting sections. It will take longer to get to these places than it will to look around and see if our marshal is there or not."

"The first is here, barely even in a sublevel, beneath the basement of this small tower," Emilie said, pointing it out on the hologram. "The tower is an import/export node, dealing with nonstandard goods going to and from the surface. Not agricultural or ore, those are processed on the other side of the station; more like luxury goods. It's been all but abandoned since the barricade went up. I don't know if we'll find anything there or not, but Curt was suspicious of some signs of activity there."

"Could just be smugglers," Geeta said.

"I did a search on the building itself, and it's not associated with any sightings of the people in black, not-quite-uniforms. So you might be correct," Emilie said. "But Curt knew most of the smugglers, the ones that worked for the Tajaki dynasty, certainly. And he didn't know anyone working out of that basement. So I left it on our list."

"Okay, what else?" Geeta asked.

"The second is far deeper," Emilie said, and the hologram moved down through sublevels until they were at the hull of the station. "It's not particularly close to the black market. Curt said it was an old, abandoned trash incinerator. I guess he saw it with his own eyes; it's not marked as such on any schematic I can dig up, back to the original rocket schematics."

"It's suspicious because it's not on the schematics?" Scout asked.

"Curt said it looked like it had been used recently," Emilie said. "He left a camera behind, but someone disabled it without him getting anything on video."

"Professionals, sweeping a room for cameras and bugs every time they go in there," Geeta said.

"Even if Liam isn't there, I'm curious if they left some evidence behind of just what they were incinerating," Emilie said.

"What's the third place?" Seeta asked.

"The back room of Club Sitara," Emilie said with a grin.

"What?" Seeta and Geeta gasped at once.

"Is that good or bad?" Scout asked.

"I don't know. Weird, I guess," Seeta said. "We go there all the time. I met Hal there, actually. It's a big counterculture hangout, but not really a shady one. It's where a lot of people put their toes in."

"Kind of counterculture light," Geeta added. "There are counterculture kids who just like the look and maybe to misbehave a little. Then there are others, mostly older ones, who we think are into more disruptive but secret activities. We've been trying to work our way up to those people, but so far we've only gotten up to the level of the Hals of the world. Not his bosses, for instance."

"But Liam might be there?" Scout asked.

"I think it's the most remote possibility of the three," Emilie said. "But Curt was suspicious that the owners had very recently been compromised and were doing things maybe not to the benefit of the movement anymore."

"Like upper management after a visit from someone dressed in black," Geeta said. "Ooh, that is interesting."

"So, what do we do now?" Scout asked. "Split up, you said. Then what?"

"Split up just for recon," Geeta said. "Anyone sees anything, call all the others and hold fast until we all get there."

"I want to take the incinerator," Emilie said. "I'm curious."

"I'll take the club," Seeta said. "I'm friendly with the staff there. I can get upstairs to the back room without drawing attention."

"Agreed," Geeta said. "Scout and I will check out the import/export building."

"Are you sure?" Seeta asked. "Did you see where it was?"

"Where?" Scout asked.

"It's behind the Enclave building," Geeta said. "I did notice. It can scarcely be a coincidence. But we'll be in the sublevels, and the only way into the Enclave is across the walkway up top. We should be fine. Plus, I took some equipment without authorization."

She stood up and took something off the back of her belt to set it on the table with a clang. It was a gun, a short-barreled gun with a large opening end.

"A grappler," Seeta said.

"What's it do?" Scout asked.

"It's for capture. Fires a sticky web that stiffens around the target, trapping them. Most people can't even keep their footing when they've been hit with one, but even if they can, there's a line that runs back to the gun, so they're tethered to me. That plus my stunner should be enough to get us out of any fixes," Geeta said. "I also have wrist comms for the rest of you. Emilie can set up a private channel for all of us."

"On it," Emilie said, taking the three new comms plus the one around Geeta's wrist and crawling back into her bunk for one of her many tablets.

Scout set the tote on the table and buckled Gertrude Bauer's belt around her waist. The loop in the back that had once held a gun was empty now, the gun still with the rebels back down on Amatheon. But she had her slingshot and a pocket's worth of stones. She put the slingshot in her back pocket, the lens and dog whistle into her left front pocket, the data disks into the little pockets on her shoes, and the stones in her right front pocket.

For a moment, it felt strange holding the stones in her hand. She had brought part of the planet up into space with her without really thinking about it. They felt heavier than normal, nestled in her palm, as if they were pulling to get back to where they came from.

It could be, in the end, these stones would be all she had to remember her home by. If she had to fire them at anyone, it would be like pelting them with her own memories in a way. It would be doubly ironic if she ended up shooting at another Planet Dweller trying to drag her back to the Enclave.

"Are we ready?" Seeta asked.

"Is the club still going to be open?" Scout asked. It was more convenient for her and Geeta to be prowling around the business after hours, and it scarcely mattered when Emilie checked out the abandoned incinerator, but breaking into a club's back room after closing sounded like an invitation to be shot as a thief.

"Club Sitara doesn't close until morning shift starts," Seeta said. "And you can always tell which of your coworkers were there all night and rolled into work in the morning on too much caffeine and no sleep."

"Club Sitara is famous for its espresso," Emilie said. "I almost wish I was going. A cup could do me good just now." Scout reminded herself that Emilie had been up all night, but for the life of her, she didn't look like she hadn't slept in nearly an entire day. She looked as fresh as she had the morning before, chowing down rice before heading to work.

"Stim?" Geeta offered.

"No thanks," Emilie said. "I've gotten by a lot longer on a lot less sleep. I'll be fine."

Scout wished she had that confidence. She felt exhausted, her brain all fogged and her hands trembling ever so slightly as she adjusted the belt around her waist.

But surely she would be all right. If anything happened, she would get that old burst of adrenaline that was ten times better than any cup of espresso. And in the meantime, she was too tired and numb to feel what should be a considerable amount of fear for what they were about to do—and all the ways it could go so very wrong.

21

THEY ALL RODE down the elevator together, but while Emilie and Seeta headed down the flight of stairs to the train level, Geeta tugged on Scout's sleeve and led the way out the front doors of the building.

Street level at just past two in the morning was eerie. All the lights were still on, but no one was about. The towers above them were largely dark as well; only a few scattered squares showed windows where the occupants within were still up. Geeta led the way along a particularly wide street with six marked lanes, but no one was driving on it.

"This is space," Scout said in a whisper because breaking the silence felt like something she ought not to do. "Why do you have daytime and nighttime here? Especially when it never gets any lighter or any darker. The entire time I've been here, no matter what hour of the day, the light level never changes."

"I gather there used to be three equal-sized shifts for a long time," Geeta said. "Families tried to stay all on the same shift, and you'd have to make friends all on your shift. I think at some point upper manage-ment was afraid people were dividing themselves into three different groups that might start squabbling with each other. They didn't want to have in groups and out groups. The mutineers on the surface were trouble enough. So they defined one daytime for everybody. Of course, lots of jobs need around-the-clock coverage, but there is a sense that when you gain seniority, you move to the preferred shift. There aren't enough people working the off shifts these days to form a group with a separate identity."

"It feels like it's been night since I left the surface," Scout said. "I miss the sun."

"I've seen it, once," Geeta said. "Well, we weren't supposed to look directly at it, but I had special glasses on. There is an observation area at the very end of the space station, the bit that doesn't turn."

"I didn't see that from the outside," Scout said. "We must have flown in from the other end."

"It's in the fore part of the ship, relative to the direction of our orbit. It used to be the command module when this was a rocket. We went there as a school trip to tour the old parts of the ship and to look at the sun."

"And what did you think?"

"It was bright, but it felt kind of cold. Maybe you need to see it through atmosphere to appreciate it."

"Maybe," Scout agreed. "I do miss blue skies. And clouds."

They walked on in companionable silence, around another corner and down a narrower street. Scout could see a walkway high over the road a few blocks down, joining two mirror-image towers. She was certain the one on the left was the Enclave.

"None of you have said anything about what Hal said. That you should run," Scout said.

"No? I guess we felt like there was nothing to say," Geeta said. "Either your friend takes us along or he doesn't."

"So you want to leave?" Scout asked.

"It sounds like it would be dangerous for us to stay," Geeta said, her jaw clenching. "They shot Hal, but Seeta was right there with him. I'm very afraid the only reason they didn't shoot her too is that they didn't know she was the one asking Hal all the questions. It did look like they were on a date, I guess. But they are capable of finding out. If your friend can't help us flee, I'll go back to the black market and find someone else who will."

"This could all happen very fast," Scout said.

"We took anything we cared about out of the apartment when we left just now," Geeta said.

"Emilie took a bag of her best tools," Scout said. "But you and Seeta, I didn't see you take anything."

"We have these," Geeta said, unzipping the front of her jumpsuit just enough to fetch out what looked like a little medallion. "Rather like your data disks, only ours contain all the images and videos we have from our childhood with our parents. Everything else up there was just stuff."

"I don't have anything of my parents'," Scout said. "It all went with the house. All I had with me the day they died was my dog Shadow, my bike, and the clothes on my back. I had to trade the bike for a bigger one when I outgrew it. The clothes too. I kept my father's hat for the longest time, but I lost it just before I left the planet, so that's gone too. Now it's just Shadow."

"He'll be with you again soon," Geeta promised.

They turned down a side street just before they would have walked between the two towers. This side of the Enclave was much like the one she had seen before, dark and featureless, with no doors or windows.

"How can they stand it in there?" Scout wondered, but Geeta didn't seem to hear.

"There it is," Geeta said, pointing to the next building after the Enclave. It was a low, squat building. The street level had no windows, but the second and third levels had massive floor-to-ceiling windows, all dark. "Empty. Good."

"How do we get in?" Scout asked.

"Through the basement. There will be an entry for deliveries in the back alley."

They crossed the street and skirted the building, ducking into the alley behind it. It was empty, not so much as a single piece of blowing trash.

It was also completely dark. Scout stopped short in confusion, but Geeta went so far as to draw the grappler, aiming it at the darker corners.

"Do you see something?" Scout asked when nothing jumped out at them.

"No," Geeta said, taking a half step forward with the gun still trained on the far side of the alley. "But there's no way that light being out is a coincidence."

"It's not?"

"No. They seldom burn out, and when they do, a notification is sent to the maintenance crew and they come out straightaway to replace it. Either it just burned out this minute or someone is tricking the system."

"So they can operate in the dark," Scout finished. "Smugglers. Maybe this place still is active. I have a light on my belt." She found the correct pouch and took out the flashlight, flicking it on and then shining it into all the shadows around them.

"The door is here," Geeta said, waving for Scout to follow her into a little stairwell that led down about a meter under street level. The stairs were wide and shallow. "You could get a hover cart down here easily," Geeta said, as if noticing the same thing.

"For deliveries," Scout said.

"Shine the light over here," Geeta said, fishing something out of her belt. Scout aimed the light at the lock on the door at the bottom of the stairs. Geeta had something like a small box in her hands. She stuck it to the door as if it were magnetic, then pushed a button on the front of it. There was a soft whir and then a beep and the lock inside the door clicked open. Geeta plucked the little box off the door and put it back in her belt before pushing the door open.

They stepped inside, Scout careful to aim her flashlight down in front of them and not flash it about. There were no windows down here, but they might not be alone. Geeta gently closed the door behind them, then led the way deeper into the cavernous basement.

There were a few crates stacked against the outer walls and some support beams that held up the ceiling but all under a very heavy blanket of dust. Whatever had been left here had gotten lost in time, forgotten, definitely not to be disturbed by anyone who didn't fancy having the mother of all sneezing fits.

"The hologram showed the sublevel under that corner," Geeta whispered to Scout. "No other entrance or exit was marked on the schematics, but that doesn't mean there wasn't one."

"Liam did disappear from surveillance close to here," Scout said. "Ready?"

Geeta nodded, raising her gun once more to lead the way. Scout aimed the light just ahead of her to light her path. Somewhere on the far side of the basement, something was glowing an electronic shade of red, too soft to illuminate anything. The only sound was their own footfalls.

Geeta reached out a hand to touch the wall in the corner of the room. There were no crates here, and no dust either. The floor was swept so clean Scout could see the faint lines left by the cleaning robot spiraling over the floor. She passed the light across the clean floor, found the line where the dusty floor behind them began, then followed that edge as far as her light would reach, back toward the front of the building.

"They don't use the back door," Geeta said.

"They're going to see our footprints," Scout said.

"Nothing to be done about that now," Geeta said and turned her attention back to the wall. "I'm not seeing anything here. But there has to be something here."

"Won't your tool open it?" Scout asked.

"Only if it's one of our locks," Geeta said. "And I'd have to know where the lock is to place it correctly."

"Hold on," Scout said, digging the single mirrored lens out of her pocket. It was even more scratched than she remembered, but it still clung ever so softly to the flesh around her eye. She closed the other eye and looked toward the corner.

"Can you see it?" Geeta asked.

"Hold on," Scout said again. She didn't want to admit that she didn't understand the tech she was using. She knew the lens could tell her things. It was just a matter of figuring out how to ask it what she needed. She stepped closer, putting both of her palms on the scuffed, cold wall and focusing her gaze just past the surface.

It felt like trying to cross her eyes, even though one was closed. But it worked. The lens sensed the outline of something behind the wall and showed it to her as a series of red lines.

"The lock is just there," Scout said, pointing. Geeta set the box on the wall and pressed the button.

The whirring went on for a long time, Geeta opening and closing her hands over and over as she waited for it to work. At last, there was a beep and a click. Geeta put the box away, then gingerly touched the wall.

It swung out toward them soundlessly, the space beyond even darker than the basement itself.

And somewhere down in that darkness, voices were arguing.

22

THE VOICES, one male and one female, were too far away for the words to be clear. They were definitely arguing, often overlapping as one interrupted the other, but neither was quite raised in full anger yet. There wasn't an echo, and even though Scout wasn't close enough to the doorway to look within, the space beyond it didn't feel immense. It felt confined. And yet there was no light.

Were the voices arguing in the dark?

Geeta started to take a step inside but put out a hand for Scout to stop. She held out her hand and Scout handed her the light, but Geeta took it only for a moment, and when she handed it back to Scout it was wrapped in a sheer red scarf, muting its brightness down to minimum usability. Scout still kept it focused just under their feet. Geeta lifted her grappler once more and took the first step inside the space.

The walls were very close on either side, and the floor slanted down before them like a gentle ramp. The voices became clearer as they crept closer, but Scout still couldn't make the sounds form words in her mind until one thing the woman said suddenly leapt out in perfect clarity.

"…Farlane McFarlane…"

Scout sucked in a breath and Geeta glanced back at her. Scout just nodded for her to continue. This was no place for even a whispered explanation about the man who went by that name. Scout had gone hunting for that man, the last criminal Gertrude Bauer had been after before she had died trying to protect Scout. Scout had wanted to capture Farlane McFarlane and bring him to her rendezvous with Liam.

And she had found him, but she had been too late. He had been shot and left dead on the floor of his hut in the middle of a wide, flat scrubland with the nearest settlement, a faint smudge on the horizon. She had taken his tablet in the hopes that it contained proof enough of his actions to entitle his victims to compensation. She still had it with her in one of the pouches of the belt. But it did no good if she couldn't get it to Galactic Central.

Farlane McFarlane had been a galactic fugitive very effectively hiding away from all human contact on Amatheon. So how did these two smugglers on *Amatheon Orbiter 1* come to know his name?

"He was never going to be reliable, not long-term," the man was saying as Geeta and Scout pressed on down the hallway.

"He was always going to double-cross us, sure," the woman said. "Only he didn't do that. He just disappeared. Why would he disappear *before* taking the biggest shipment of his life? If he wanted to pull one over on us, he would have taken it and *then* run."

"He said he was a wanted man. Maybe he wasn't lying. And his past caught up with him."

"I still think he's dead," the woman said.

"Either way, he's no use to us now. And he was our only route to the rebels on the surface besides Malcolm Haley, and he's not answering either."

"Perhaps the whole planet died, and no one told us."

The man made a scoffing sound.

Geeta clutched Scout's arm to signal for her to stop. Scout froze, pulling the light almost entirely behind her. That left only the faintest glimmer of reddish light to illuminate Geeta as she slowly crouched, turning toward the wall.

Not the wall, Scout realized as her eyes picked forms out of the darkness. There was an opening. Geeta glanced up at Scout, once more signaling for her to stay where she was. Scout nodded and Geeta put a foot down into the opening. It was like there was another hallway below, perpendicular to the one they were in and about half a level down. Geeta looked up at Scout again, her chest now at the level of Scout's feet, and signaled for her to wait there. Then she crept ahead, quickly disappearing into the darkness.

Did the hallway descend in a series of switchbacks, or maybe just keep circling around to wherever the smugglers were talking? Scout had no clue.

"We're going to miss having the constant feed of information from him, that's for sure," the woman said.

"He was becoming more and more unreliable," the man said.

"That's because you kept jacking around his dosage," the woman said, all but cutting him off. "He was so unstable, he was nearly useless."

"I had to jack the dosage or he would've plateaued," the man said. "And you're right, he was getting useless, so what difference does it make we can't control him anymore? We had him long enough to learn not only was he not the one in charge, he wasn't even in high command outside of his own fevered imaginings."

Scout's wrist comm vibrated, too softly to make a sound, but she felt it. Someone was trying to contact her, but she wasn't sure if there was a way to dim its screen to check the message. She didn't want to risk flaring the space up with light just in case there was a way the two people below might see her.

If Seeta or Emilie were calling Scout, then they were also calling Geeta, and Geeta would know how to see the message without being seen. Scout should just wait.

Which was nearly unbearably frustrating.

"We should send someone down to the surface," the woman said.

"You volunteering?" he asked.

"No way. I'm supposed to be moving up from radio watch soon."

"I don't know, taking the crap mission to the surface might be a fast track to a better position," the man said. "I might do it myself. It would certainly beat waiting around here for the Months to decide to make a move."

Scout frowned. That last bit didn't make any sense. Her mind was sensing a capital letter on *Months*, but what would that even mean? Hal had always said he worked for "the bosses." Did the people in black work for an organization called the Months?

She jumped as a hand closed around her ankle but didn't make a sound, just bent to help Geeta get back up into the hallway. Geeta waved for her to follow back up the ramp to the basement. She swung the door closed behind them with a click but still put a finger to her lips and headed out the back door to the alley.

"What's going on?" Scout asked, still whispering, although there were now two heavy closed doors between them and the two who had been talking.

"It looked like some kind of communication room. Lots of equipment, computers monitoring transmissions all over Amatheon and in orbit, to judge by the labels on the screens. I guess they're there in case the computer finds an interesting one it wants human ears to listen to. But it was a tiny room, nowhere to hide Liam, and no other way out. He wasn't there. And the two people chatting were wearing jumpsuits with some fashion modifications. Not the black sort of uniforms. Maybe counterculture, but I didn't recognize either of them. They were older than us, though. Older than Hal even. But maybe not counterculture or Curt would have known them, right?"

"Who are the Months?" Scout asked.

"One of many questions I now have," Geeta said, then looked down at her comm. "Seeta says he's not at the club either. That means either Emilie is on the right trail or we start over from square one."

"Let's get to Emilie," Scout said.

"Okay, come on. The nearest train station is this way," Geeta said. She set a brisk pace that didn't slow as both of their comms vibrated again. She tapped the screen as she walked, Scout moving closer to hear the conversation.

"Malini here," Geeta said.

"Something's wrong with Emilie," Seeta said breathlessly. "She answered my call a minute ago and said she hadn't found anything yet, but her voice cut off mid sentence and now she isn't responding at all, not even with text. I'm on my way there now."

"No, stay where you are. We're already on the way," Geeta said.

"Okay," Seeta said, a bit taken aback by the urgent command in her sister's voice. "Did you find anything at the import/export building?"

"Not Liam," Geeta said. "We heard some other things we're going to want to dig into later. The people in the subbasement weren't in black not-uniforms, and they seemed to be tied to someone called 'the Months.' They had a man down on the surface, but apparently he's dead now."

"He is," Scout said grimly.

"Everyone here is really spooked," Seeta said. "The club owners are acting jumpy, and people who have been longtime regulars are not showing up. Some of the waitstaff think there might be foul play. I think it's more likely that the change in the vibe of the place has them hanging out elsewhere, but we should look into it when we can."

"How *is* the vibe?" Geeta asked.

"It's not the old Club Sitara anymore. It feels like the cafeteria at school when the headmistress came in to eat with us."

They had reached the stairs that led down to the train platform, but Geeta stopped. Scout could hear the sound of someone walking below. Geeta tugged Scout's sleeve and pulled her deeper into the shadows just beyond the stairwell. Then she leaned in close to the comm to whisper to her sister. "We're closer to Emilie than you are and we're already on our way. Why don't you sit tight and wait for word from us? We might need to have someone topside to run for backup."

"I'll go into the security building then," Seeta said, also whispering. "I left my log from my last shift unfinished, so I have a reason to be there, anyway. You call for help and I can send the entire squad out to extract you."

"Perfect," Geeta said. "We're about fifteen minutes away. I'll text when we're there."

"Thanks. Stay safe," Seeta said. "You too, Scout."

"Will do," Scout said.

The train was just rolling away when they reached the platform and without a word they both started running, swinging onto the little grate behind the last car and holding on as the train gathered speed and plunged them into the darkness of the tunnel.

23

AT THE NEXT STOP, they hopped off the grate and got inside the last car of the train, to Scout's relief.

"How far?" Scout asked as Geeta examined the glowing map on the train car wall.

"This is our line. We ride it all the way to the end," Geeta said. "Twenty minutes."

"That long?" Scout said. "If she's been hurt—"

"We're getting there as fast as we can," Geeta said. "Seeta couldn't get there any faster."

Scout nodded glumly. Liam and Emilie both missing, maybe hurt, maybe worse. She was too fidgety to stay in her seat and got up to pace the length of the train car, such as it was.

Geeta rolled her head back against the window and fell fast asleep. Scout knew this was more about how exhausted Geeta was than anything. It didn't mean Geeta wasn't just as anxious to get there as Scout was. Still, having to wait all alone with nothing but her own fears on a loop in her mind for company was hard.

"End of the line," the voice over the speaker announced. Scout turned to nudge Geeta, but she was already awake, blinking hard as she got to her feet.

"Alright?" Scout asked.

"Well enough," Geeta said. They exited the train car but lingered on the platform until the train had left. "I'm not exactly sure where the opening is," she admitted.

"I'll find it," Scout said, pulling the mirrored lens from her pocket. She kept both eyes open as she jumped down to the tunnel floor. It was a little disorienting, but it was too dark to rely on just one eye. She scanned the walls around them as they walked to the very end of the tracks.

"I should have grabbed a copy of the schematics for my comm files," Geeta mumbled.

"No need. It's just there," Scout said, pointing up. There was a shaft that opened up in the space between two unusually close-together support beams. It was hidden in the shadows, but now that she knew it was there, she could see the outlines. The floor of the shaft was at chest height, and she pulled herself up and stood.

It was a long, narrow hallway. When she looked up, she couldn't see the ceiling above them, not even with the lens. It was like they were creeping along a gap between two of the space station compart-ments. A flaw in the design? Or did they have to leave space for the space station to flex, maybe? She didn't know much about engineering. Emilie probably knew.

"This runs straight to the incinerator," Geeta said, grappler once more in her hand. "I remember that from the specs. Can you see in the dark with that thing?"

"Yes," Scout said.

"Then let's do this quiet and dark. I'll follow behind you, but if you see anything, just drop down in a hurry. I'll hear you moving and fire. Got it?"

"Got it," Scout said. But just in case, she had her slingshot in one hand, a stone ready to fire in the other.

Scout walked as silently as she could down the long corridor, placing one foot after the other carefully. She couldn't hear Geeta behind her at all, but resisted the temptation to look to be sure she was still there. She could count on Geeta.

The floor near the walls was dusty, but the center was mostly clean. People walked down this way often enough to wear a path.

The walk went on even longer than the train ride, and Scout's eye started to ache from trying to compensate for the differences in what they were seeing and what her lens was telling her.

The lens was detecting something ahead of them, but it was so distant she didn't know what the brighter spot she was looking at meant. She wanted to rush forward, but what if there were other things behind that spot? She had to wait for more information.

The bright spot gained an outline, kind of bundled and low to the ground. The lens was giving her a temperature reading. The bundle was warmer than the rather chilly air of the corridor. It was 36°C. A person running a little cooler than normal?

Then the lens detected something else: an array of dots all around the corridor, clustering up ahead in a larger space. Cameras, watching them. She turned and looked back. They had passed one camera already, but the corridor beyond that was clear.

Geeta's eyes were wide and questioning, the pupils huge in the darkness, but Scout couldn't answer her. She put a hand on her arm and squeezed, then pushed her gently back. Geeta nodded, her face grim, and started moving backwards step by step without turning around.

Scout crept up to the bundle on the ground. There were actually two bundles: a bag of tools that was the same temperature as the corridor had been lurking behind the outline of Emilie's body on the floor. Scout put the bag over her shoulder, then grasped a fistful of the back of Emilie's jumpsuit and dragged her back past the last camera. She continued as far down the corridor as she could before the load just got too heavy and she had to let Emilie go.

Emilie whimpered, and Geeta gasped, just realizing what Scout had been dragging. Scout grabbed Geeta's wrists and brought them down until she could grasp Emilie around the shoulders. Then Scout took her feet, and they quickly got her back out to the very edge of the corridor. Light from the train platform lit up a wedge of the space and they helped the waking Emilie sit up in it.

"You're bleeding," Geeta said, opening a pouch on her belt and pulling out a little spray bottle. Emilie let Geeta tip her head to one side, hissing as Geeta pulled the hair behind Emilie's ear back from the cut across the top of the growing lump at the back of her skull.

"Did you see him?" Scout asked.

"No," Emilie said, hissing again as Geeta sprayed something over the cut. It had a medicinal, almost plasticky smell. "That's cold," Emilie complained.

"There were cameras all over down there," Scout said. "They must have seen you go in. They hit you when you were one camera in. Their response time is crazy fast. We should get out of here."

"No, I don't think they'll bother to come back," Emilie said. "They don't know it was just me who found their hidden whatever. They'll consider the location burned and abandon it."

"Let's get back to the platform just to be on the safe side," Geeta said. "I want to be under the watchful eye of station security."

"Can you walk?" Scout asked.

"I think so," Emilie said, but then less comfortingly she added, "My hands feel huge. So that's weird."

Scout hoped that was random strangeness from the mind of Emilie Tonnelier and not a worrying sign of a brain injury.

Geeta helped Emilie get down and cross the tracks and then get back up onto the platform. A boy about their age was waiting on one of the benches, but if he thought it was odd that they emerged from the dark tunnel, he didn't show it, just looking them over as if to see if he knew them and, when finding he didn't, completely ignoring them.

Geeta settled Emilie on a bench as far as possible from the boy and took another look at the lump on the back of her head now that they were in better light. The adhesive was binding together the broken skin, but the lump was sizable.

"Should we get her to a medical pod?" Scout asked.

"We should go back in there, look for clues," Emilie said. Her voice was firmer now, but her eyes were still scarily unfocused.

"No, I agree with Scout. You need medical attention, and we should connect with Seeta and decide what the next step is."

"I didn't see Liam, but I never got all the way in to the incinerator,"

Emilie said. "What if I just barely missed him? They might have been there and seen me coming. They can't have gone far."

Scout thought of how long it had taken them to get to Emilie, how far they had traveled in that time. "They could be anywhere by now." She showed Emilie the chronometer on her comm.

"I was out that long?" Emilie said, flinching as she touched the lump with her fingertips. "I've got blood in my hair."

"Train's coming," Geeta said. "We should head to security."

"No," Emilie said, beckoning at Scout repeatedly until Scout realized she wanted her bag. She set it down on the bench next to her and Emilie pulled out her heavy-duty tablet, tapping the temple of her glasses and running her hands over the tablet with dizzying speed.

"What are you thinking?" Geeta asked.

"They didn't get to do what they went down there for," Emilie said. "I interrupted them, and they were gone when you went down there or they would have attacked you, too."

"I will agree that they've gone," Geeta allowed.

"Let's assume they fled before completing their task," Emilie said through gritted teeth, either from pain or annoyance at Geeta's hair-splitting, Scout couldn't tell. "I can figure out where they'd go next to finish the job."

"But there was only once place down there that Curt flagged," Scout said.

"He was flagging places where he noticed signs of activity he couldn't account for," Scout said. "They set up cameras around that incinerator because that was their go-to incinerator. Now that it's been compromised, they'll need another. A place they haven't used before, so Curt wouldn't have flagged it."

"But you said the incinerator wasn't marked on any of the schematics," Geeta said.

"It wasn't, but now that I know what to look for..." She sat back, hands hovering in the air over the tablet. Little squares of light were winking on around the schematic that filled the display.

"So many," Scout said.

"We start with the closest," Emilie said, zooming in. "It's just a short walk the other way in that train tunnel."

Geeta looked up at the waiting train. The boy had gone into one of the train cars and was spinning around one of the support poles, kicking his feet up in the air with each rotation, clearly bored out of his mind.

Scout wondered what that felt like.

"All right," Geeta agreed. "We'll go down and check it out. But what are we going to do if we stumble upon another network of cameras? Scout can detect them with her lens, but how do we get past them without being seen at all?"

"I can see them with my glasses too, now that I know to look out for them," Emilie said a bit defensively. "And I have a little toy that will short them all out at once."

"They'll know something's up," Geeta said.

"So we move fast. But we were going to do that anyway, right?" Emilie said, and that old maniacal grin was back on her face.

Geeta frowned in thought. The train slowly pulled away from the platform, the boy within still spinning and doing high kicks.

"Alright," she conceded. "I'll text Seeta that you're okay and tell her where we're going. But at some point, this is going to get dangerous enough where we'll want to call in Sergeant Murray and the team. I don't trust upper management, but I trust Sergeant Murray. Once we're safe, we can deal with the political ramifications of all this if we have to."

"They'll have us in chairs for days, answering questions," Emilie said. "We'll be punished for every little infraction we've broken since I started breaking into buildings when I was eleven. We'll likely be sent out to one of the tiny, weightless stations for the rest of our careers. Apart."

"Maybe," Geeta allowed. "But we won't be dead."

24

EMILIE LED the way along the train tracks, scanning the wall with her glasses as she walked, the camera-destroying device clutched in one hand like she might need to throw it at any time. Scout followed behind, Emilie's heavy bag of tools over her shoulder. She had left the lens in place over her left eye, even though the eye strain was giving her an ever-worsening headache. She didn't want to walk blind.

Geeta, bringing up the rear with the grappler in her hands, was going to be blind the moment they started down the shaft. If that thought bothered her at all, she didn't show it, just walked on with her mouth one thin grim line.

Emilie climbed up into another shaft hidden in the shadows between two closer-than-normal supports, and Scout surmised there must be quite a number of them dispersed along the tunnel. The light from an approaching train was growing stronger around them and Geeta darted off the tracks to stand close to the wall, out of obvious sight from the train driver. Scout handed up Emilie's bag and climbed into the shaft, Geeta following behind her just as the train passed, filling the shaft with a cold wind that caught loose strands of Geeta's hair and spun them around her head.

Scout touched her own, shorter hair. Whatever Rudolf had sprayed it with before he left was keeping it smooth and flat against her head, even in the wind, although it felt a little crusty now. She tried not to count the days since her last shower.

Emilie slung the strap of her bag across her body and cinched it close to her side, then led the way down the tall, narrow corridor.

This one was dustier than the other, and the dust clearly showed a row of fresh footprints. Two were from boots with heavy treads, one set significantly larger than the other. A third set of footprints was very scuffed, as if the walker had been dragging their feet. Or as if the other two had been doing the dragging, pulling him along between them.

Him. Scout didn't want to hope, but she couldn't help it. Was she almost back with Liam? Almost on her way out of this place?

Emilie paused when the first tiny, easy-to-ignore dots appeared in Scout's lens. Her glasses might have better detection, or just looking through both eyes helped. She adjusted the object in her hand, then threw it like she was pitching a ball as hard as she could as far as she could.

There was an abbreviated clatter, as if it had struck something but then stuck fast. Scout looked up at all the cameras. Her lens was still detecting them, but she didn't see any way to tell if they were functioning or not. Emilie turned back and gave her a thumbs-up before jogging on down the corridor.

That was as sure as things were going to get, Scout guessed. She gripped her slingshot and rock in her hands and ran after Emilie. She could hear the sound of Geeta following behind her.

Emilie stopped at the end of the corridor just out of the light from the room beyond until the other two caught up. A man and a woman were in the room, clearly looking around to figure out where the clattering noise had come from. Scout took in every detail of the space she could in the flickering light. A long tube-shaped machine dominated the back wall, the bottom a grill with a fire beyond, which was the only source of light. She didn't see Liam in any of the shadowy corners of the room; where was he?

"Forget it, we have a job to do," the man said and abandoned the search to start pushing the buttons on the machine. "Stupid thing—why is it so slow?"

"It's been cold for centuries," the woman said. Her voice had a strange accent to it, but her leather pants and long black cloak were all too familiar.

But where was Liam?

Geeta pushed past Scout and Emilie and fired her grappler. A long white mass streaked out of the end, expanding into a glimmering web large enough to contain both of them. It hit the man square in the chest and immediately contracted to wrap around him, but the woman had twisted out of the way and was rolling across the floor.

"You," Geeta said as the woman sprang back to her feet, her black cloak whirling around her. She had a gun in her hands and raised her arm to aim it at Geeta, but Geeta didn't give her the chance, charging across the room to tackle the woman to the ground.

Emilie kicked the man in the net away from the controls and started typing madly. Scout realized why she was in such a rush when she finally saw where Liam was: already in the machine, head lolling back and forth and moaning but not quite conscious even as the space around him was rapidly heating up.

"We have to get him out of there!" Emilie said, pounding away at the button to turn off the heat. The machine was ignoring her.

Scout took half a step toward the machine. But something made the hairs on the back of her head prick up and without a thought she turned, fitting stone to slingshot in one smooth, long-practiced movement, and fired back down the corridor.

Someone yelped in pain and fell to the floor.

Scout doubted she had more than momentarily dazed whoever it was, but it would have to do for now. She ran up behind Emilie, took a long, sturdy wrench out of the bag at Emilie's hip, and jumped on top of the machine to pound at the apex of the curved window.

"It's jammed!" Emilie said as Scout kept raining down blows. The impact was jarring all the way up to her shoulders, but she couldn't stop. Then Geeta and the woman in black, locked in tight combat, fell against the machine, driving someone's elbow into the side of Scout's leg and sending her sprawling. She couldn't stop her fall in time and she slid headfirst between the wall and the far side of the machine, only managing to twist enough to meet the floor with her shoulder rather than the top of her head.

"There's another in the hall!" she called as she scrambled back to her feet. Geeta and the woman had separated and were circling each other. Geeta had her stunner in her hand. The woman was looking for an opening to dodge past Geeta to get to her fallen gun.

Then a man with blood streaming down his face from a fresh wound on his forehead came charging into the room. He ran at Emilie, who had her back to him as she bent over the control panel with a tool, removing the panel to get at the circuits behind it.

Before Scout could shout another warning, Geeta saw the man and spun, catching him around the shoulders from behind and pressing her stunner under his jaw. He twitched, his eyes rolled back, and he fell to the ground. Geeta let him drop, lunging in the direction of the fallen gun, but both it and the woman in black had disappeared.

"Got it," Emilie said, ripping something out from behind the panel. The flames sputtered and died away. Then they were in darkness. Scout fumbled to get her light off her belt and peel away the red scarf. Emilie had turned on the lights from her glasses as well.

"We still have to get him out of there," Scout said as she climbed back over the top of the machine. All of her blows hadn't even scratched the glass.

"Er... I might have just ripped that bit out too," Emilie said, examining the back of the panel with a frown.

"I've got it," Geeta said, taking her lock-breaking device out of her belt and setting it over the edge of the lid. This lock was nowhere near as sophisticated as the others; the device beeped almost at once and the click echoed through the narrow room.

Scout lifted the lid, then flinched back from the sudden rush of hot air.

Emilie swore as she, too, pulled away. "No one could live in heat like that."

"He might," Scout said, peering over the rim of the machine. His hair, eyebrows, and eyelashes had all been singed away, and his skin was all oozing burns, but his chest was still slowly and sporadically rising and falling. "He's not awake, but he's breathing. Can we get him out?" She climbed on top again, reaching under his shoulders to hoist him up to a sitting position.

"How is he possibly okay?" Emilie asked, as if seeing the impossible annoyed her to anger.

"Nanites, I think," Scout said. "Galactic marshals are a sturdy bunch. Otherwise, they would have cut his throat before dragging his body down here to be incinerated."

"They did cut his throat," Geeta said, sounding a little sick. Scout rolled Liam's head back. Then she felt sick as well. His nanites must have healed him over and over again, so many lines crisscrossed his throat.

"Help me get him down," Scout said, rolling him onto his side so that he dangled over the edge of the incinerator, arms swinging as if he were reaching for the floor. Emilie and Geeta pulled him out into the room as Scout hoisted his legs after them until they had him sprawled across the floor.

The very cold metal floor. The touch of it on his sweat-soaked body was the shock that finally roused him. His eyes fluttered over and over before finally opening. He looked at Emilie in her dark glasses and Geeta with the stunner still in her hand with confusion, but when Scout jumped down into view, the relief that washed over his face was so profound Scout felt tears pricking at her eyes.

"Sorry it took so long to find you," she said. "But we got here just in time."

Liam summoned a very weak smile, barely more than a twitching of his lips, but when he tried to speak, all that came out was a wordless croak.

"His throat," Geeta said.

"His skin," Emilie said, holding up her hands covered with clear pus. "It broke open everywhere I touched him."

"It'll heal," Scout said, hoping she was right about that.

"We should get moving," Geeta said. "This one will be out for a couple of hours, and that other one isn't going anywhere until someone dissolves the grappling net, but the woman got away."

"Back up the corridor?" Scout asked. It was going to be hard enough getting Liam back up that narrow space without worrying about running into an ambush.

"No, I don't think so," Geeta said. "I was standing right here with this fellow. Her gun was over there, nowhere near the door."

"I don't see another way out of here," Emilie said, scanning the room through her glasses.

"That opens onto space," Scout said, pointing to the other end of the incinerator.

"I don't see how she could have gotten out that way so quickly, let alone survived in the vacuum. Unless she has something in common with your friend here," Geeta said. The three of them all shuddered at once, hating that idea. That would mean she was all but unkillable.

"Ship," Liam said, the word just intelligible.

"We have to get out of here first, then get to Seeta," Geeta said. "Then the dogs, then the ship. And we'll have to hurry. If that woman went to get her allies…"

Geeta let the end of her sentence drop, but only because explaining what they all knew would be a waste of time. She pulled Liam to his feet, wrapping one of his arms around her shoulders. He had to walk with a bit of a stoop, as short as she was, but he didn't seem capable of straightening all the way up yet, anyway.

Emilie led the way at a half jog, head swiveling constantly as she scanned for hidden dangers. Geeta and Liam limped along behind.

Scout came last, walking backwards, slingshot and stone ready in her hands, unable to shake the fear that the woman in black had blended with the shadows, hidden even from Scout's lens and Emilie's glasses, watching them hunt for her escape route and waiting for them to let their guard down to spring her attack.

Whoever she worked for, she definitely wasn't from Amatheon, the surface, or the orbiting stations. She was galactic.

25

THEY WAITED at the end of the shaft for the train sitting at the platform here at the end of the line to fill with passengers. Liam slumped against the wall, eyes closed, but he was by degrees looking better. Scout glanced from his pale face to Geeta's ashen one and realized he was already nearly looking better than the exhausted ensign. Well, more alert, anyway. His skin was healing, if still an alarming shade of red, but the lack of hair was disturbing.

The train rolled closer, and they fell back into the shadows. Scout wasn't sure if anyone looking out the window would be able to see them—no one seemed to have noticed the existence of the shafts—but it was best not to take chances.

She looked back again, back the way they had come, but as far back as her lens could penetrate, nothing was moving.

She wished she found that reassuring.

"Come on," Geeta said, hopping down to the ground and reaching up to help Liam follow. "It's getting on six and people are heading to their work shifts. The next train will be here in minutes."

The tools in Emilie's bag jangled together as she landed. Scout put her slingshot and stone away and jumped after the others.

The walk back to the platform seemed longer this time. Perhaps

Liam was slowing them down, although Scout was starting to feel exhausted herself. She was running on too little sleep and she was beginning to feel the effects, her feet stumbling even where there were no obstructions.

She took no comfort in the knowledge that Geeta undoubtedly felt worse.

The light from the platform ahead was growing brighter, but not as quickly as the light from the approaching train behind them. Geeta spoke close to Liam's ear, encouraging him to fall into a shuffling jog. Emilie ran ahead to spring up onto the platform, then turned to extend her hands to the others. Scout bent her head and forced herself to quicken her pace.

There were dozens of people on the platform, all staring at them as they pulled themselves up out of the tunnel and collapsed onto benches. They only got to sit for a few seconds before the train pulled up and the doors opened. Geeta herded them all into a middle car and stood at the door, glaring at other potential passengers until they opted to ride in one of the other cars. The sight of Liam beyond her looking an absolute wreck made a nice backup to her "you don't want any part of this" nonverbal argument. The doors at last hissed shut, and they were alone.

"Where are we going?" Emilie asked as she slumped in one of the seats. All of her ebullient energy seemed gone, and her eyes were just barely open.

"The landing platform?" Scout asked hopefully. "Get the dogs, get out of here?"

"The ship isn't there anymore," Geeta said. "It was impounded and moved."

"Where?" Scout asked. Liam's eyes were fixed on Geeta; he had the same question.

"I'll find out," Emilie said, forcing herself to sit up higher and taking her tablet out of her bag.

"I should check in," Geeta said. "There has to be a way to get someone down there to pick up those two for questioning without implicating us, but my head is just too full of bees to figure out how."

"Oh no," Emilie said, her voice grave. Geeta, hand still hovering over the comm she hadn't touched yet, looked up.

"What is it?" she asked.

"Is there a problem with the ship?" Scout asked.

"They saw me," Emilie said, her voice shaking. "The people in black. They saw my hair."

"What does that mean? Are they coming to find you?" Scout asked, but from the look on Geeta's face, she was missing something.

"What have they done?" Geeta asked.

"There's a lot of chatter on the counterculture nets," Emilie said. "Things are happening all over."

"What—" But before Geeta could finish her question, her comm started beeping at her, loud and not to be ignored. Plus, the train was rolling into the next stop. Geeta shot Scout a glance and then turned to deal with her comm. Scout planted herself in the doorway and summoned her fiercest scowl. She had words at the ready too, but didn't need to utter any of them. One look at her and everyone waiting on the train platform hustled to fill the other cars.

"It's going to get too crowded for that to keep working," Scout warned as the doors finally closed and the train moved on.

"The black market is on fire," Geeta said. "People in black are boiling up out of every dark alley and executing anyone showing signs of being with the counterculture. There is violence all over."

"Because of me," Emilie said. "They think I did this as part of the movement."

"Don't blame yourself," Geeta said sternly. "They've mobilized so quickly I can only assume they were only waiting for a signal."

"Or an excuse," Scout said.

Geeta's comm chimed again. Scout stepped closer as Geeta opened the line.

"Geeta?"

"Seeta. You're okay?"

"Yes, I'm fine," she said, but her voice hitched over the word. "I just saw an alert go out over the security network. The owners of Club Sitara blocked the doors and set fire to the building with everyone trapped inside. They are trying to put out the flames now, but it doesn't seem like..." She choked back a sob and took a deep breath. "You're okay?"

"We have Liam and we're on the move," Geeta said. "Emilie, do you have a location on the ship?"

"Impound hangar 47-H," Emilie said. "We'll need to change trains at the next stop."

"Did you hear that, Seeta?" Geeta asked.

"47-H. I'll grab the dogs and meet you there," Seeta said. "I can't believe this is really happening. Are we really leaving?"

"We have to. Seeta, be sure to cover your hair," Geeta said.

"I did that before coming into work," Seeta said.

"Are you going to have trouble getting out with the dogs?" Scout asked.

"It's bedlam around here. No one is going to notice me doing anything," Seeta said. "If I leave now, I'll probably beat you there."

"We'll move as fast as we can," Geeta said, but even making the promise looked like it took something out of her, the black rings under her eyes darkening.

"Stay safe," Seeta said and was gone.

Geeta went to the door of the train car and pressed her face to the glass to look ahead. She opened a pouch on her belt and took out a little injector the size of her thumb. She unzipped her suit enough to bare the top of her shoulder and press the injector against her skin. It triggered with a snap that made Scout jump, but Geeta didn't even flinch.

"Anyone else need one?" she asked. "Emilie? How's your head?"

"I'll be okay," Emilie said. She had taken a knit cap out of her tool bag and tucked all of her candy-red hair underneath it. Her face, without that garish frame, looked younger, like a little girl wearing her dad's enormous glasses while she played dress-up.

"I'm mending," Liam said distinctly, although his voice was still hoarse. "Just point me in the right direction and I can run if necessary."

"We're getting off at the next stop and changing platforms. I don't know what we're going to find. It could be like an ordinary day, like the last platforms were. It could be violence and chaos. Scout, cover your hair."

Scout reached up, feeling the cut ends of her hair. It was only delicately orange, not quite an improbable color, but Geeta's voice said she wouldn't be entertaining any objections. Scout loosened the scarf tied around her neck and brought the back of it up over the top of her head. Geeta reached out to try to brush the bangs back from Scout's forehead, but Rudolf's spray was tenacious stuff. She pulled a fold down lower over Scout's head, then arranged the ends around her shoulders so it looked like a fashion statement and not a hasty disguise.

"Here we go," Emilie said, getting to her feet as the train rolled into the station.

Scout looked at the faces of the people waiting on the platform. They looked anxious, nervous, but no one here was fighting. They must have heard reports, too. They were as afraid for what they would find happening on the train as Scout was afraid of what might be happening on the platform.

"Come on," Geeta said, leading the way out of the train car. Emilie followed, hoisting her bag back up onto her shoulder. Scout gave Liam her arm. He was walking with more strength now, but she suspected his talk of being able to run might still be a bit too optimistic.

The stairs led up to an atrium filled with people hurrying from gateway to gateway, people selling steaming cups of coffee, and a plethora of screens all showing videos of the fire at Club Sitara. Geeta skirted the crowd that had gathered to watch the news and led them down another staircase to a different platform. Scout helped Liam to sit on one of the benches against the wall.

"Did we lose Emilie?" Scout asked when she straightened back up.

"No, I'm here," Emilie said, pushing something soft and warm into Scout's hands. She peeled back waxed paper to reveal a steaming croissant split down the middle to hold a cooked egg and a disk of some sort of vat meat.

"How do you do that so fast?" Scout asked, her mouth already full.

"Skill," Emilie said, handing a similar package to Geeta and another to Liam. "Sorry I couldn't carry four coffees too, but no time to run back now. Here's the train."

Geeta stuffed the last of her sandwich in her mouth as she took a step closer to the train. Her hand behind her, fingers splayed wide, was telling the others to stay where they were. A murmur was rolling through the crowd gathered between the benches and the train that turned into cries of alarm and anguish when the doors slid open. The crowd rushed back, people fleeing off the platform and back up the stairs until only Geeta remained facing the open doors of the train.

Every passenger in every car was dead, sprawled out on the floor in puddles of blood.

"Throats cut," Liam said hoarsely.

"Counterculture kids, all of them," Emilie said.

"Come on," Geeta said, her voice hard. "This is our train."

"But—" Scout started, but she quailed under the fierce gaze Geeta turned on her.

They had no other choice.

Emilie adjusted her bag and then reached out a hand to help Liam to his feet. He pointed at her bag, and she turned until he could pull the long wrench free, the one Scout had tried to use to free him from the incinerator. He slapped it against his palm and followed Geeta onto the train.

Emilie reached up and pulled off her knit cap, tousling her bright red hair until it stood all on end, a swirl of chaos around her grimly set face. Only then did she board the train. Empty-handed but ready to face anything.

Scout took out her slingshot and followed. She could do no less.

26

SCOUT STEPPED onto the train and began to help Geeta and Emilie move the dead bodies out of the car before the doors closed. The smell of blood was still so thick in the air it clung to the back of Scout's throat like she was sucking on a piece of metal. They all remained standing, even Liam, although he clung to a support pole as the train picked up speed beneath them, jostling its passengers sporadically.

Geeta's comm sounded another alert, but she just shut her eyes and ignored it. Emilie stepped closer to her, unfastened it from Geeta's wrist, and made some adjustments, then put it back on. Scout guessed it was a line to and from Seeta only now.

Scout found herself pacing between the two doors, looking out at the walls passing in a blur. How many had it taken to kill all these people? How long? Between one platform and the next?

Where had the attackers gone?

Emilie was staring fixedly at the ceiling of the train car now as if wondering the same thing. "Maybe it's time to break some of the big rules," Emilie said.

"What do you mean?" Scout asked, but Emilie didn't answer. She pulled her tablet out of her bag and sat down on the floor to type with both hands. Her eyes behind the glasses were darting madly back and forth, and Scout could only imagine the amount of information she was processing and navigating through.

Geeta opened her eyes to look down at Emilie, her face impassive. Emilie lifted both her hands in silent triumph, the maniacal grin back on her face.

"What did you do?" Scout asked.

"Overrode the train system," Geeta said as the train beneath them started rocketing even faster across the station. "Like Sergeant Murray did when we had to get you to the Enclave in time for the meet. We're running at maximum speed, making no stops, and the other trains are giving way."

"Neat trick," Liam said.

"If anyone is on the outside of the train waiting for some special signal to attack, I hope I've just made holding on for dear life the most they can do," Emilie said.

"No one is here but us," Geeta said. "Why would they stick around? No one else was ever going to board this train. They would have to assume it would be empty."

Scout could see the logic, but the feeling that some menace was lurking all around them, waiting to spring out at them the moment they let their guard down, didn't fade.

Several minutes later, the train began to slow, then it stopped at a platform that was little more than a walkway extending a handful of meters past the bottom of a flight of stairs. They all got out without a word and climbed the stairs. As they climbed, they tripped motion sensors on the lights, and when Liam at the end of their line stepped off the platform, the lights there snapped off.

"Is this normal?" Scout asked. It was creepy having the station sense their position and provide a bubble of light just for them.

"This hangar is for impounded vehicles. Most of them have been here for decades. No one visits," Emilie explained. "There are other parts of the station like that. Energy-saving feature for a minimal-use area."

And then there were spaces like the incinerator rooms with no lights at all. Scout supposed this was preferable to that.

The stairs ended at the edge of a long, narrow hangar. Opposite the stairs was an enormous window looking out into space. A wedge of Amatheon was visible rotating around the perimeter.

Then Scout noticed a soft blue glow to that window and realized it wasn't glass between them and the vacuum of space. It was some sort of field.

Ships were parked in a row on both sides of the stairs, but most of them were tiny, holding little more than a single pilot with maybe a bag stowed under the seat. But others were as lovely and strange as Liam's ship, gleaming beautifully and delicately shaped but still recognizably ships. Others were stranger still. She wouldn't have even taken them for ships if they hadn't been sitting out on what was clearly a flight deck. One in particular, a collection of bubbles that sat in a quivering pyramid, caught her eye. The bubbles were large enough to hold several people each, but their transparent surfaces danced in rainbow colors like any ordinary bubble from soapy water.

How was that safe in space?

"There's my ship," Liam said, his voice still a bit croaky. He started to walk toward it, but Emilie grabbed his arm.

"You can't take off from there," she said. "The landing gear are locked down. The system has to tow you to face the launch window. We have to get to the command room first."

"Where's the command room?" he asked, and they all scanned the walls around them. There was a catwalk halfway up the wall, high enough to offer a view over the tops of even the tallest of the ships.

"Seeta!" Geeta cried and started running across the hangar.

Scout saw Seeta waving from a window overlooking the hangar. Then she saw a black dog's head appear, paws on the edge of the window, a little white dog repeatedly jumping into the air, and she was running too.

Seeta dropped to one knee to hold both of the dogs by their collars as Geeta and Scout burst into the room. At first, Scout was afraid they didn't recognize her. Her clothes, her hair—nothing about her was the same as it was when they saw her last.

But the minute the door was closed and Seeta released them, they ran straight to Scout, barreling into her and knocking her over. Shadow was barking happily, trying to smell every inch of her. Gert was wagging her tail so mightily her entire back end was propelling back and forth.

"I missed you guys," Scout said, burying her face in the fur of Gert's neck as she hugged the squirming Shadow close.

"I tried to move the ship to the ready position, but the system wants an access code," Seeta was saying. Geeta went to the window to wave for Emilie and Liam to hurry up and join them.

"Any trouble getting out here?" Geeta asked.

Seeta's face fell. "I got through okay," she said, but the shaking of her voice said there was more to it than that. She had a story to tell, but now was not the time.

"Access code," Geeta said as Emilie came in the door.

"On it," Emilie said, pulling out her tablet.

Liam stayed just outside the door, either keeping guard or just unwilling to be out of sight of his ship.

"It's moving," Geeta said.

There was a sharp rap against the window, Liam knocking to get their attention. Scout thought he was just confirming that his ship was being towed by the cable attached to its nose, slowly moving to the center of the hangar, but from the looks on the faces of Geeta, Seeta, and Emilie, that wasn't what was going on. Scout pushed the dogs off her lap and got to her feet.

People in black not-uniforms were all over the hangar, running up the staircase from the train platform below, stepping out from behind other ships, leaping down from the catwalk that encircled the space. Dozens of them, all heading toward Liam and the command room.

"We can barricade ourselves in," Seeta said.

"We need to get to the ship," Scout said.

"It's time," Geeta said and lifted a plastic cover to press a large red button set in the wall near the door.

"They'll get here too late," Emilie said. "If they get here at all. They are already swamped dealing with everything that's happening up above."

"We need to get to the ship," Scout said again.

The other three exchanged looks, having the sort of nonverbal conversation only sisters or very old friends could conduct. Then they all looked back to Scout and nodded.

Scout threw open the door and went out to stand beside Liam, slingshot at the ready, her dogs at her heels. Geeta stood at his other elbow, grappler in her hands. Emilie saw a bin of tools next to the door and helped herself to a wrench twice the size of the one Liam was brandishing. Seeta had found something even better: a needle gun. Whether she had found it in the command room or taken it with her from the security building, Scout didn't know.

The people in black had closed in to form a ring just out of the reach of Liam's wrench. They parted to let the woman in the swirling black cloak step forward.

"This is only going to end one way," she said. She had no weapon in her hands.

"You know that I don't know anything about your situation here," Liam said. "You could not have been more thorough with your interrogation methods. Just let us go."

The woman tipped her head to one side, her sleek black bob swinging with the motion. "But you do know something now. A clever man would deduce so many things just by the questions I asked, and I know you're a very clever man."

"Killing me to keep me quiet isn't going to work out for you," Liam said. "I'm a galactic marshal."

"Who not only has no jurisdiction here, but was specifically ordered not to pass the barricade."

"A dead marshal is still a dead marshal. Do your employers really want the heat that will bring?"

The woman shrugged with a carefree smile on her lips.

"Who are you people?" Emilie demanded.

"Lay down your weapons and surrender to us and perhaps we will tell you," the woman said.

"Before or after you slit our throats and incinerate us and scatter our ashes into orbit?" Scout asked.

"We only want this one dead," the woman said, pointing at Liam with a finger ending in a long, black nail like a talon.

"Then why did you murder so many of our friends?" Emilie asked.

The woman shrugged. "We can't be blamed for all of that. Some of it wasn't even us. Call it collateral damage," she said. Emilie lunged for her, but Liam caught her arm before she could swing her wrench at the laughing woman's head.

"We have to fight," Scout hissed through her teeth. "We have to get to that ship."

Suddenly both of the dogs started barking at once, Shadow's attention-seeking yips as well as Gert's deep hellhound woofs. Some of the people in black fell back a step, but the woman just looked down at Gert with an indulgent smile.

"What set off the puppy?" she asked in the sort of voice some people used to talk to babies or animals.

"Probably them," Geeta said.

The woman's eyebrows drew together in mild curiosity. She grinned like she was indulging Geeta's whim, then looked over her shoulder to where Geeta had been pointing. Squads of navy-blue jumpsuits were erupting from the top of the stairs, stunners at the ready as they charged across the hangar.

"Oh, goody," the woman said, her gun suddenly in her hand. "This *is* going to be interesting, after all."

27

SCOUT FIRED her slingshot at the woman, but she was already gone, the ends of her cloak fluttering behind her as she ran to meet the newcomers. But her stone was only one of many projectiles suddenly filling the air. The people in black had dart guns like the one that had killed Hal. They also had needle guns like the one Seeta was firing and even more conventional guns.

"Get down!" Liam shouted, pulling Scout behind the hull of a small ship. The dogs ran to cower beside her. Seeta had fired her gun dry and ducked back into the command room to reload. Geeta was struggling with one of the people in black, her grappler fallen at her feet, but Emilie's wrench made short work of her opponent and they, too, headed for cover behind another nearby ship.

"The ship is in position," Scout said, peeking around the side of the landing gear she was hiding behind.

"We just need to find a way to get to it," Liam said. "Run for the command room. We'll have more options there than pinned down here."

Scout nodded, tucking her slingshot away. She tried waiting for a lull in the fighting, but there didn't seem to be any moments that were better than the others. In the end, she just kept her head as low as she could and sprinted for the open doorway.

The dogs figured out what she was doing and blew past her to the safety of the room. Liam was right behind her. Then Geeta and Emilie ran in, having seen them go by, and Geeta slammed the door shut.

"I thought barricading ourselves in here was a bad idea?" Emilie said to Liam.

"We can't stay here long," Liam said. "We have to make a run for the ship. It's our only hope."

"How?" Geeta said. "We won't make it more than ten meters before something hits us."

"Wait for the fight to die down?" Emilie suggested.

"Since they both want us in custody, it's hard to pick which one to root for," Scout said.

"The one that won't murder us," Geeta said.

"Just give it a minute," Seeta said. "Things are about to change."

"What do you mean?" Scout asked.

"I called some friends," Seeta said. "They're on their way, and they're fighting mad."

"How many can be left?" Emilie asked.

"Enough," Seeta said. "A lot of us were killed in the first moments, but the word spread fast. I know there's something odd about that woman, how fast she moves and how she seems to walk through walls, but most of those people in black are just like us. Completely killable. These here are likely the only ones left on the whole station, at least from what I've been hearing."

They all looked out the window at the fight on the hangar deck. The guards had the advantage of numbers but were having trouble because they were bottlenecked at the top of the stairs. The woman in black was moving fast as a blur from one of her people's position to the next, hands pointing as she gave orders before zipping on to the next.

"Who is she?" Liam wondered. "Who does she work for?"

"If they all focus on the top of the stairs, we could maybe slip behind them to get to the ship?" Scout suggested.

"They'll see us," Emilie said.

Then, as if on cue, something flew through the air, spewing

smoke behind it as it drew a slow, lazy arc. It hit the ground and then quickly disappeared in a cloud of eye-stingingly thick smoke.

"They're on the catwalk," Seeta said, pointing. Scout looked up to see a dozen or so counterculture kids, many of them already bloodied and bruised from other fights, all of them tossing smoke grenades down onto the hangar deck.

"They're giving us cover," Emilie said. "It's now or never."

Liam threw open the command room door and ran for his ship. Tired as she was, Scout easily overtook him. She had until recently spent every day of her life on a bike, pedaling over hill and prairie. It might actually have felt good, running full out after so many days with so little exercise, but the smoke-filled air burned her throat and made her eyes run.

The dogs, closer to the ground where the fallen grenades were still spitting smoke, liked it even less. But they stayed close to her, ears flattened back and eyes wide with fear. Scout knew just how they felt. Bullets and darts were whizzing by, some close enough she could swear she felt a stirring of air against her skin, but she couldn't stop. If she stopped running, she might never start again. She'd just be paralyzed with fear, hiding behind some ship that was never going to take her away from all this.

Scout and the dogs reached the ship first, and she slammed her hand on the mechanism to lower the ramp and raise the door. The process was as painfully slow as ever. She turned to see Liam just emerging from the overlapping clouds from two grenades. Geeta and Emilie were close behind. Emilie had found another needle gun somewhere and was firing it towards the top of the stairs. She couldn't possibly know if she was even hitting anything or which side was taking her fire.

The counterculture kids up on the catwalk were yelling and cheering. They had run out of grenades but had other objects they were raining down on the combatants at the top of the stairs. Scout guessed on a space station, where stones weren't conveniently lying around waiting to be thrown, you picked up whatever else you could find. Tools, dishes, knives of all shapes and sizes. Someone was even hurling full bottles of jolo that exploded in furious bursts of sticky carbonation.

As soon as the ramp touched the ground, the dogs scurried up into the ship. Shadow's tail was tucked so far between his back legs he was walking with a stooped shuffle, staying close to Gert's side.

Liam ran up after them to get into the pilot's seat and get the ship running.

Scout stayed at the bottom of the ramp, waiting for the others. Emilie's needle gun was out of needles, so she flung it into the smoke and ran for the ramp. Geeta stopped a few meters away, grappler dangling from her hand as she searched the clouds of smoke for any sign of her sister.

Then Seeta came stumbling out of the haze, running backwards and firing at someone behind her.

The woman in black. Needle after needle was embedding itself into the flesh over her heart, but she paid them no heed. Her hands were once more empty, but as soon as she emerged from the smoke and had a clear view of Seeta, she raised her arm and pointed her wrist at Seeta. Seeta threw the now-empty needle gun at her but she batted it away, only momentarily dropping her aim.

"Seeta!" Geeta cried and started to run towards her sister.

A beam shot out from the woman in black's metallic gauntlet. It hit Seeta like a cannonball, lifting her off her feet and propelling her through the air, bent double with arms and legs dangling nervelessly.

She hit the hangar deck a dozen meters away with a sharp cry of pain, her body collapsing like a floppy doll. But she still had momentum, far too much momentum. She skidded across the floor, straight through the force field that separated the atmosphere in the hangar deck from the vacuum of space. Her scream cut off, its sound no longer able to reach them.

"Seeta!" Geeta yelled, charging toward the force field. Seeta was just on the other side, but she was tumbling further away by the second. Geeta raised the grappler and fired.

The white substance passed through the force field and stabbed out into the vacuum beyond. Its net unfurled in ever-growing spirals.

But none of the tendrils reached close enough to Seeta to catch her.

"No!" Geeta shrieked, falling to her knees.

Scout saw the woman in black behind her, preparing to fire that weapon again and push Geeta out the opening to join her sister. Scout drew and fired her slingshot in one motion. She didn't have time to aim, but years of practice didn't let her down. She hit the woman square in the forehead and the woman fell back on one knee.

She wasn't going to be down for long. Scout ran to Geeta's side to pull her to her feet.

"We can still get her with the ship!" she said, pulling Geeta towards the already-rising ramp. The two of them stumbled on board, Emilie there to pull them clear of the closing door.

And just like that, all the smoke and noise of the fight was gone.

Scout scrambled to her feet to get to Liam's side. She was just in time to see the force field break over the windscreen.

"Hold on!" Liam cried, but his warning was too late. It was like the space station had had enough of them and was flinging away the ship as far and as fast as it could. Liam had buckled into the pilot's seat, but the rest of them tumbled about the cabin. Scout hit her head on the back of Liam's chair and struck the ceiling hard enough to knock her breath out, then felt something pop in her shoulder as she somersaulted into the back wall.

Then Liam got the ship under control and the rest of them were floating gently. Emilie was clutching her head, eyes shut tight. Shadow and Gert were both whimpering.

Geeta looked beyond shocked. Her whole body was shaking, and she was making a low moaning sound as she hugged herself.

"Seeta!" Scout cried, pushing off the back wall to grab on to the back of Liam's seat. "Can you get to her?"

"There she is," Liam said, guiding the ship after the tumbling body.

"How can we get her inside?" Scout asked. They couldn't just open the door.

"There are controls here," Emilie said. She was blinking hard, wincing still at the pain in her head, but her face was all focus as she pulled herself into the passenger seat. Unlike Scout, when Emilie looked at the panels in front of her, she had a clue what they did.

"Can you…?" Liam's voice trailed off as he focused on his flying.

"Yes," Emilie said. She touched one of the panels and it rotated, providing her with a pair of controls like handles. She grasped them, twisting and pivoting them as she stared fixedly at the screen under her feet.

"There she is," Scout said as Seeta came into view. She was already icy white and still. A pair of metallic hands came into view, their motions mimicking Emilie's on the controls. They deftly caught hold of the edge of Seeta's lavender scarf and tugged her close enough for the hands to close around her in a firmer grip. Then the hands retracted back out of view, taking Seeta with them.

"I have to get us further out from the space station," Liam said. "There's a hatch..."

"On it," Emilie said, getting up from her seat and finding the control to open a hatch in the floor between the two seats.

Under the hatch was a small space, no bigger than a locker, but large enough to hold Seeta. Scout helped Emilie pull Seeta out to float free inside the ship. Her body was already so cold it hurt to touch her. She was stiff. Her hair was frozen in a whorl around her head.

There was no way she could be anything but dead.

28

EMILIE PRESSED her hands to Seeta's cheeks, touched the sides of her neck, then her wrists, as if searching for a pulse. But Seeta wasn't a piece of tech she could figure out just by examining it. She looked at Scout helplessly.

"Liam?" Scout asked.

"Kinda busy here," Liam said. "They're coming out after us."

"Who's coming out after us?" Scout asked.

"I don't know, but they're good," Liam said, his mouth a grim line. "Get everything secured. I'm going to have to do some fancy flying to evade these guys."

Emilie was already pulling Seeta to the back of the ship. Scout remembered where things were from her earlier search of the ship and opened the largest of the cupboards, packing both of the terrified dogs inside. She didn't think there'd be airflow if she shut them inside, so instead she found a roll of repair tape and made a mesh she hoped would be strong enough to last until they were out of this mess.

Dogs secured, she finally looked around to see how the others were doing. Geeta was still hugging herself and moaning, despite Emilie's attempts to get her attention. Seeta's body was wrapped in a plastic sheet and tied to the back of the passenger seat with the rest of the cord Scout had used for the dogs' leashes.

Scout pushed away from the wall just as Liam banked the ship around. The motion sent her tumbling into Geeta and Emilie and she got a fistful of each of their clothing to keep the three of them together until the ship went back to steady forward motion.

"I don't see any sign of injury, but she's catatonic," Emilie said.

"Shock, maybe," Scout said. "Let's buckle her into the passenger seat. If she's not going to hold on when we change velocity, we can't have her getting hurt, or hurting Liam."

Emilie nodded, catching the back of the chair with her foot and towing them all close enough for Scout to get a handhold. Geeta was staring unseeingly at the world around her but allowed herself to be pushed back against the seat and strapped in. Scout caught her arms, tucking them under the belt across her chest.

"Hang on," Liam said again, and a sudden burst of speed pulled everything to the back of the ship again. Scout tried to keep her hold on the back of the chair but only ended up twisting her wrist painfully before tumbling after Emilie.

The dogs were whimpering.

"What can we do?" she asked. She wasn't sure if she was talking to Liam or the universe at large.

"My codes won't get us through the barricade anymore," Liam said. "We're stuck here."

"Back to Amatheon?" Scout was startled to find herself relieved at the thought of going back. At least she understood that life. It hadn't been such a bad life.

"We can't go anywhere until I lose the rest of these pursuers," Liam said. "They're good, but they're flying junk. By the time we get around to the far side of the planet, we'll be out of visual contact of all of them."

"Then what?" Emilie asked.

"Then I go dark," Liam said. "This ship will disappear from all tracking systems. After that, they won't know where we've gone."

"How long can we just tumble through space?" Scout asked, but Liam didn't answer, just fired another burst of speed.

"What can we do for Seeta?" Emilie asked Scout. "There must be something."

"I don't think it's hopeless," Scout said. "We lost a lot of escape time retrieving her. Liam wouldn't have risked that if there wasn't some glimmer of hope."

She thought about Gertrude Bauer, the other galactic marshal she had known. The nanites coursing through her body had made her all but indestructible. Liam had them, too. Gertrude had cut one out of her own body to save the life of a cat. Scout didn't think for a moment that Liam would do any less for a human.

And yet, was it too late? The cat had been seriously hurt, but he hadn't been dead yet.

"Should we warm her up or keep her cold or what?" Emilie said. Her anguish over not knowing what to do made Scout's heart ache.

"I'm sorry, I just don't know," Scout said. She pulled Emilie into a tight hug, holding onto the edge of the dogs' cabinet with her other hand to keep them both from spilling away as the ship took another banking turn and burst of speed.

"Okay, this is my opening," Liam said. "Hold on."

Scout hugged Emilie tighter as the acceleration increased to an almost unbearable crushing power.

And then it was gone. They were back to floating.

"Where are we?" Scout asked, pushing back to the front of the ship.

"We're on our way to the far side of the planet," Liam said, watching a screen that seemed to be showing the view behind them. There were a few tiny points, very distant ships barely visible in the darkness. Then they were gone.

Liam flipped a switch and let out a long, shaking breath.

"They can't find us now."

"They might, eventually," Scout said. "You said we can't cross the barricade. So, are we going back down to the surface?"

"Can we hide there?" Emilie asked.

"Maybe, but I don't want to risk it. It's so closely watched," Liam said.

"So where then?"

"I was thinking the far side of Amatheon's moon," he said. "No one has ever used it for anything. I don't think anyone will look for us there. If they do, we'll see them coming and can outrun them again."

"How long can we hide there?" Scout asked. "Are we going to run out of air?"

"No, we won't run out of anything. But I can send a signal from there to my friends back home. They'll do what they can to help," he said. He sounded infinitely tired.

"And what about Seeta?" Emilie asked.

"Can your nanites help her?" Scout asked.

Liam looked surprised by the question. "No, it's too late for that. But I have a stasis kit. It's possible she can be revived back at Galactic Central."

"Possible?" Emilie repeated.

"I don't want to make promises I can't deliver on," Liam said. "I can only promise I'll do all I can. I'm not a medical doctor, I don't know all the factors involved. I just know sometimes they come back."

"Thank you," Emilie said grudgingly.

"If you want to watch the controls here, I'll get the stasis kit and get to work. Just watch for anything unusual. It's going to be an hour or so before I alter course for the moon."

"Okay," Emilie said.

Liam unbuckled from his seat and drifted to the back of the ship. Emilie took his place, looking over each panel carefully. By the time Liam came back, Scout was sure Emilie would know as much about his ship as he did.

She looked at Geeta, still staring numbly ahead of her. Her hands had come free from the belts, but she had folded them together. The shaking was just in those hands now.

"I missed," Geeta said, not looking at Scout.

"You had no time," Scout said.

"I had enough time," Geeta said. "My mind was running so fast. Because of the stims. I could see every angle. I knew just where to aim, how to pull on the net to get her back inside without getting hung up on the edges of the opening. I was compensating for the spin of the station, everything. I had it all worked out."

She stopped, looking down at her hands, and Scout was afraid she was going to go back to the low moaning. But she didn't. She unfolded her hands and spread them wide, fingers splayed. They shook. Scout saw Geeta make a deliberate effort to hold them still, but still they twitched.

"I missed because I couldn't stop the shaking. Not for a single second. I only needed a second," Geeta said. She turned her hands over, forming tight fists. Scout knew the grief must be overwhelming in a way that even she, who had lost her baby brother on the same day as her parents, couldn't really understand. But Geeta shed no tears.

"We might be able to bring her back," Scout said softly.

"Might," Geeta repeated.

"I know it's not much. But it's all we have."

Geeta nodded. Scout didn't know what else to say. Geeta felt like she needed to shield herself off from hope. Who was Scout to tell her to feel differently?

If she thought for a moment it would help at all, she would confess her own feelings of guilt. Geeta's hands had been shaking because of all the stims she'd been taking because of *Scout*. Helping Scout around shifts of pretending to look for Scout and getting no sleep. But Scout's blame was on an even more fundamental level than that.

The sisters and Emilie would be together right now in their little apartment happily eating butter chicken or drinking insanely rich, sweet tea or planning little insurrections if Scout had never left the planet's surface.

But Scout knew the last thing Geeta needed while dealing with her own grief and feelings of guilt was to have to make Scout feel better about hers. So she said nothing.

But she couldn't push that feeling aside. It was going to be her companion for a long, long time. It might not go away even if Seeta got better. It certainly wouldn't if she died.

29

AMATHEON'S MOON wasn't much to look at from the surface. It was tiny, just a slightly brighter point of light than the stars beyond it, moving across the sky just fast enough for you to observe if you were bored and willing to stare at it long enough. Scout had done that herself many times, spread out under a tent of prairie grass waiting for sleep to take her.

But Amatheon's moon, seen up close, was quite fascinating. Not exactly beautiful, but unforgettable. Red bands squiggled over the otherwise beige surface, looking from the distance like a fertilized egg with a chicken just beginning to form inside, one band with a blot of darker scarlet that looked like an eye. Other bands joined together like a network of veins.

As they drew nearer, more details emerged. Scout had the stomach-churning realization that what it most reminded her of was when she had once seen the badly sun-damaged scalp of an old man who had spent a lifetime never wearing a hat. The repeated sunburns had left scars and cancerous spots. The moon's surface looked like that.

But then the blots became mountains and the veins long canyons, and Scout could force gross biological imagery out of her head and focus on the geological formations.

They circled the moon several times as Liam looked for the best spot to land. Finally, he settled on a wide plain that looked like it had been a bed of lava once ages ago but was now dust-covered glass of a reddish-black color. He set the ship down.

"No gravity?" Emilie said as she found herself still bouncing in the back of the ship.

"Some gravity, not much," Liam said. "It's just a little thing, your moon."

"Now what?" Scout asked.

"Now I make sure the space station is on the far side of Amatheon and then send that message off to my friends. After that, we eat."

"And after that, we wait," Emilie said with a sigh.

Dinner was meat loaf with gravy and a side of potatoes, which they sucked out of packets with little straws built into them. Inelegant, maybe, but warm and filling. Liam helped Scout fashion diapers for the dogs, who still didn't know what to make of life in microgravity. She was worried they weren't getting enough water since they found drinking from bulbs too odd.

She hoped they wouldn't be here long.

Liam and Geeta slept in the seats in the front of the ship. Emilie and Scout curled up in little hammocks they made out of blankets, Scout with both dogs tucked up beside her.

It felt so good, to just sleep and sleep. To be safe. To have her dogs with her.

She woke in the morning to find Liam listening to a message over his earpiece, his face intent. Geeta and Emilie were already awake, watching his expression for clues as they sucked at packets of oatmeal. Scout raised her eyebrows questioningly, but the two shook their heads, unwilling to speak until Liam was done.

At last, he took the piece out of his ear and set it in its spot on the console. He floated to the back of the ship to help himself to one of the packets of oatmeal, and Scout took one as well. She pulled the cord to activate the heating cell and cupped her hands around it to feel the growing warmth against her palms. It was colder in Liam's ship than it had been back on the space station, and she had never felt quite comfortable there.

"Someone is coming for us," Liam said. "I can take you all to Galactic Central. I would love nothing more. But I need you to understand what that means."

"People are going to want us dead," Emilie guessed.

"Yes," Liam said. "People like that woman in black back at the hangar. People who are very good at making sure the people they want dead die. My friends and I will do everything we can to keep you safe, but they are very concerned that you know and understand that everything we can do might not be enough. And they want you to know all your options."

"We have options?" Emilie asked.

"I can take you back to your station," Liam said. "I can drop you off at one of the other stations. I can leave you on the surface of the planet. Once they arrive, I can even leave you here on the far side of the moon with everything you'd need to live out your days inside a colonizing structure. You'd be safe, but you'd be alone. I can't speak to what could happen to you in the other situations. Perhaps you can guess. I don't know."

"I think we want to go," Emilie said, looking to Geeta.

"I hope that's what you choose, but there's more you need to know."

"More than someone wanting to kill us?" Emilie asked.

Scout started to laugh but saw that Liam's face was deadly serious. "Worse than someone wanting to kill us?" she asked.

"My friends need your help. And the help they need… it's not going to be easy." He took a deep breath. "I don't know how much you know about the history of this place."

"We descend from the crew of the colony ship *Tajaki 47*," Emilie said.

"Yes," Liam said. "But by the time your ancestors arrived here, they were no longer in contact with the Tajaki dynasty. They went about their colonizing without active input from anyone back home. And you've had your problems since then, war or mutiny or whatever."

Emilie and Geeta nodded along with his words.

"What you may not know is the reason for the silence." He looked at them questioningly, and they looked at each other and then shook their heads. "The head of the Tajaki dynasty died shortly after the colony ship reached Amatheon. He died suddenly, leaving no clear successor. His descendants have been fighting over the empire he left behind from that moment to this, for centuries, with no clear winner. But it has broken down into two about equally powerful factions. They have wrestled over every possession until one or the other was victorious in securing it. I believe Amatheon is the last of those possessions. And so the fight has descended upon you."

"The people in black," Emilie said.

"The barricade," Geeta added.

"Because there are two sides," Scout said. "So which side captured you? And why?"

"That I don't know. It probably doesn't matter in the big picture."

"The woman in black," Scout said. "She has modifications. Nanites, like you. But she kept cutting your throat even though she knew that wouldn't kill you."

"Some of that was for torture," Liam said. He rubbed a hand over the top of his head where the first short, fuzzy growth of hair was just starting to come in.

"But she knew what would, didn't she?" Scout asked. She touched her own back, just where her kidney was. Where the assassin girl had stabbed the otherwise unkillable Gertrude Bauer. "Why didn't she?"

"She was the only one there like her," Emilie guessed. "She didn't want them to know."

"Possible," Liam said. "But if she works for the Tajaki dynasty, if they made her into what she is, she is something far beyond what I am."

"Maybe no weakness?" Scout asked. Liam just shrugged. But something else was still bothering her, another thing that made no sense. "The girl assassins," she said.

"Yes, you mentioned them before," Emilie said. "I wanted to ask what you meant, but we sort of got swept up in other things."

"There were three I know for sure down on the surface," Scout said. "I suspect there are more. Girls of about twelve, with modifications, trained to kill. I'd been led to believe they were planted there by Space Farers to take out Planet Dweller government officials."

"I've never heard a thing about that," Emilie said. "No rumors, nothing when I was digging around computer files."

"So, who is creating them? The people in black or the group that's been smuggling things? And why?"

No one had an answer. At last, Liam broke the silence. "I still have to tell you about my friends. They were born on a world much like yours, a colony that was neglected for centuries until the Tajaki dynasty heirs arrived to fight for ownership. The people on their world didn't even know they were living on a planet that belonged to anyone besides themselves.

"They had prospered while forgotten, but then the Tajaki dynasty took over. The people became little more than slaves. Technically free, but with no one able to afford to leave their home world, they had no choice but to work for whatever wages the Tajaki dynasty deigned to give them. And all the resources of the beautiful world they had thought theirs were now being exploited for the good of the Tajaki dynasty coffers."

"That's going to happen here," Scout guessed.

"And we're even less prepared to fight it, sounds like," Emilie said.

"That might have been true, but it's not true now. You have allies, allies who want nothing more than to take the Tajaki dynasty down a notch. They lost their world, but you might still be able to hold on to yours, and they want to help you do that. But it means testifying in a Galactic Central court. That can be an arduous experience, on top of the dynasty trying to silence you by killing you."

"But when it's done, we'll be free," Emilie said.

"*If* you win your case. Which can take years."

"Years," Scout repeated numbly. She had no idea what testifying in a court meant. It could be more than she was smart enough to do, having abandoned school at so young an age. It certainly sounded like something better-educated people did.

But she had no other plans.

"I'm in," Scout said. "All I ever wanted was to leave this place. That hasn't changed."

"We'll be in the floating cities, won't we? The seat of government in Galactic Central?" Emilie asked. Liam nodded. "Then I'm in." She rubbed her hands together, saw Scout looking at her in confusion, and broke into a wide grin. "Libraries of information. More than I could possibly absorb in a lifetime. That's all *I've* ever wanted. That and to hold our leaders accountable for their actions, of course."

"I'm in," Geeta said.

"And I'll do all I can for your sister," Liam promised.

"I know you will," Geeta said, her voice as cold and hard as ice. "But more than that, I want to take them down—all of them." She balled a hand into a fist in front of her mouth, as if swearing on it. Scout was pretty sure Geeta was picturing a certain woman in black when she made that vow.

Liam went back to his chair to message their responses to his friends.

Friends.

Scout looked at Geeta and Emilie working together to tidy up from their little meal. As horrible as everything that had happened had been, not the least of it being thrown off the walkway, it had all been worth it to Scout. She had never had friends before, except her dogs. Now she had three.

She looked out over the desolate landscape, across the blood red plain with its feathering of dust like ash. The mountains in the distance bit into the sky like jagged teeth. It fit her mood.

Because if the number of her friends should drop, Scout would be right there with Geeta and Emilie, swearing to take bloody vengeance on the entire Tajaki dynasty. She doubted they would be afraid of a bunch of teenage girls with no skill for violence, but someday they would be women, strong, dangerous women.

And that day was not so distant anymore.

CHECK OUT BOOK FOUR!

The Travels of Scout Shannon continues with book four, Against Impassable Barriers.

Stranded on the far side of the moon with her friends, Scout Shannon waits for rescue from galactic central. Hunted by two sets of enemies, surrounded by an impenetrable barrier maintained by an almost alien class of humans, time runs short.

Caught between two factions of a powerful trade dynasty, Scout fights to remain free and to protect her friends. But the people trying to make her their pawn barely seem human to her eyes. Fight them? She can barely understand them.

With friends on both sides of the planetary blockade, Scout just needs to find a way to get her friends stuck on the inside to those waiting for them on the outside.

But foes also lurk on both sides. And they hide among her friends. How to tell friend from foe? Scout better learn before the enemies close in around her.

"Against Impassable Barriers" the fourth book in "The Travels of Scout Shannon" series, a young adult science fiction novel for fans of resourceful heroines, political intrigue, and loyal dog sidekicks.

Against Impassable Barriers, book four in the Travels of Scout Shannon. Check it out!

NEW SERIES: THE FORGOTTEN PLANET

Coming soon from Ratatoskr Press Books, the new YA sci-fi series THE FORGOTTEN PLANET starts with book 1: Raiding the Forgotten Derelict.

History sleeps beneath them all, but only she sees it.

Lafayette Eloi always knew her parents thought differently from others. They kept their books buried beneath her mother's house. They spoke an old language in the dead of night, whispering behind closed doors and bolted shutters. She grew up in a village where no one was related to her, and she never knew why.

Then, after her mother died, her father came to fetch her. Now she and her mother's dog assist her father in his work. The work discussed in whispers in the dark. The work that had cost Lafayette so much all her young life.

But now she learns just how much her father's work means to their entire world. Only no one knows anything about it. Only her father. And only Lafayette.

Because the work that consumed her father's entire life and her mother's too now nibbles at the fringe's of Lafayette's own life. And she cannot refuse its call.

Raiding the Forgotten Derelict, first book in the new YA sci-fu series THE FORGOTTEN PLANET, available in September 2024 from Ratatoskr Press Books.

COMPLETE SERIES: THE RITCHIE AND FITZ SCI-FI MURDER MYSTERIES

The Ritchie and Fitz Sci-Fi Murder Mysteries starts with Murder on the Intergalactic Railway.

For Murdina Ritchie, acceptance at the Oymyakon Foreign Service Academy means one last chance at her dream of becoming a diplomat for the Union of Free Worlds. For Shackleton Fitz IV, it represents his last chance not to fail out of military service entirely.

Strange that fate should throw them together now, among the last group of students admitted after the start of the semester. They had once shared the strongest of friendships. But that all ended a long time ago.

But when an insufferable but politically important woman turns up murdered, the two agree to put their differences aside and work together to solve the case.

Because the murderer might strike again. But more importantly, solving a murder would just have to impress the dour colonel who clearly thinks neither of them belong at his academy.

Murder on the Intergalactic Railway, the first book in the Ritchie and Fitz Sci-Fi Murder Mysteries.

COMPLETE SERIES: THE TRAVELS OF SCOUT SHANNON

The complete six-book series THE TRAVELS OF SCOUT SHANNON begin with book one, Under Falling Skies.

Scout Shannon's whole family died the day the Space Farers dropped an asteroid on their domed city. Now she lives alone, out in the wild with only her dogs for company. She prefers it that way.

But Scout finds herself at a crossroads. One road leads back to a quiet life snug under the protective dome of a city. The other road leads to a life in the rebellion, a life of adventure and excitement but also danger. Dare she try to find the rebels hiding in the hills?

Then a chance encounter with a stranger from the other side of the galaxy threatens to derail what remains of Scout's life. The entire galaxy awaits her, if she survives the next four days.

"Under Falling Skies", a young adult science fiction novel, set on a remote planet with a distinctly Old West feel. For fans of gunslinging women and young girl assassins. And dogs.

Under Falling Skies, the first book in THE TRAVELS OF SCOUT SHANNON, available everywhere now.

SCI-FI SERIAL PODCAST!

Check out my new monthly podcast of serialized science fiction: THE TALES OF THE CHAI MAKHANI TRIO!

Elyot loathes the massive Commonwealth ships that hover menacingly over his home world of Adghal. He hates the Commonwealth enforcers who harass the populace even more. But with his mother missing and presumed dead, Elyot keeps his head down and strives to avoid notice. And he succeeds until the day two strangers enter his life...

New episodes of this sci-fi serial drop every 1st of the month.

Now streaming on Apple Podcasts, Google Podcasts, Spotify, Stitcher and more. Also available in eBook and print everywhere books or sold. For a complete episode listing, check out the page on my website.

ALSO FROM KATE MACLEOD

Love heists and capers? Then check out my new series, THE VIC HARPER CAPERS. The action starts with the novella THE THIRD POLE JOB.

Vic Harper and her gang retired wealthy from their life of thievery and heists. Whether in a luxury condo overlooking the river in Minneapolis or in a modernist mansion built into the side of a mountain in Colorado, life comes easy now.

Perhaps too easy.

When an old friend asks for a favor his niece, Vic and her mentor Chase Woodward leap at the chance to relieve a little of the boredom. But a quick bit of B&E in a wealthy suburb of Chicago leads to an even greater challenge.

The prize? Nothing much. Just the opportunity to level a playing field for their friend's niece.

But the heist? May prove to be their toughest ever. Because to get to the prize, they'll have to climb a mountain.

And not just any mountain. Their prize waits on the summit of Mount Everest.

THE THIRD POLE JOB, the first novella in the Vic Harper Caper series. For those who love capers, heists and other impossible missions.

Or like murder.

The complete series is out now, and it all starts with Charm School.

FREE EBOOK!

Like exclusive, free content?

To get two prequel short stories to THE RITCHIE AND FITZ SCI-FI MURDER MYSTERIES as well as a bonus prequel novelette to the completed six-book series THE TRAVELS OF SCOUT SHANNON, signup for my monthly newsletter at KateMacLeodWrites.com.

Thank you!

ABOUT THE AUTHOR

Photograph © 2016 Jonathan Conklin

Kate MacLeod has written stories which have appeared in Analog, Strange Horizons and Mythic Delirium, among other places. She is also the author of two young adult science fictions series: The Travels of Scout Shannon, and The Ritchie and Fitz Sci-Fi Murder Mysteries. She also contributes to a serialized science fiction podcast called The Tales of the Chai Makhani Trio. She currently lives in Minneapolis, Minnesota.

Find out more about the author and sign up for her newsletter at KateMacLeodWrites.com.

ALSO BY KATE MACLEOD

Novels

The Slums of the Solar System:

Mitwa

The Mars of Malcontents

The Whole World for Each

Books 1-3 Box Set

The Travels of Scout Shannon:

Under Falling Skies

In Quaking Hills

Among Treacherous Stars

Against Impassable Barriers

Over Freezing Altitudes

At Galactic Central

The Travels of Scout Shannon Books 1-3

The Travels of Scout Shannon Books 4-6

The Travels of Scout Shannon Books 1-6

The Ritchie and Fitz Sci-Fi Murder Mysteries:

Murder on the Intergalactic Railway

Murder in the Skies

Body in the Catacombs

Death on the Summit

An Undiplomatic Murder

A Lethal Betrayal

The Forgotten Planet

Raiding the Forgotten Derelict (Forthcoming September 2024)

Sci-Fi Novellas

The Intergenerational Tree

I Rise into a Daybreak

Caper Novellas

The Third Pole Job

The Twelve Days of Christmas Job

10-Story Collections

Tales of Blood and Ink

Tales of Old Gods and New

5-Story Collections

Tales from Heian-Kyo and Others

Tales from the Edges and Ends

Tales from Forgotten Days

Tales from Ancient and Future Times

<u>Tales from Across Space</u>